# SOMETHING NEW

## A HOLIDAY SPRINGS ROMANCE

B. IVY WOODS

## BLURB

**A jilted bride and an overwhelmed banker from New York are about to embark on the adventure of a lifetime that neither of them had seen coming. Sometimes love happens at the most unexpected times and places.**

Romance writer, Nicole Ford, always believed in happy endings. Until her own groom left her standing at the altar. Determined to make her own happiness, she sets off for their romantic honeymoon at Holiday Springs, alone.

Barrett Pierce, an investment banker from the Big Apple, may have gotten himself in a little hot water and needs to take a break before he's in too deep. Fleeing to the mountains, he has one plan - clearing his head and figuring out a way to fix his mistakes.

Neither of them was looking for romance, but they sure found each other and discovered a passion they couldn't ignore. Forget something old, and something blue...this time, these two love-birds have found something brand new.

**Escape to the romantic paradise of Holiday Springs and warm up with your next happily ever after.**

*To Alicia, you are a life saver and I don't know what I'd do without you.*

ONE

NICOLE

**A Few Months Ago**

*SLAM.*

I watched as my phone fell to the floor. I knew I could have scrambled to get it, but I was frozen in place. I was lucky I hadn't dropped the drink he had just given me too.

"Could you say that again?" I asked, giving him a chance to repeat the words I already knew he'd said. But maybe if he said it one more time, I would be sure I wasn't losing my mind.

"I don't want to get married."

I glanced around the room before looking back at my newly minted ex-fiancé. I then looked down at his clothes, the black tuxedo with a single white rose boutonniere, created to match my bouquet. His entire ensemble was something that we'd chosen together for what was supposed to be our special day. One glance out the window confirmed that the rain, which had been predicted, had started as the droplets hit the windows of my hotel suite. It had also figuratively moved inside to this very room.

My hands moved down to my waist and tightened the belt of the white silky robe. It was something my mother had bought for me several weeks ago. The creator had stitched the word *bride* onto the back of it, another reminder of what was supposed to be happening today. The other reminder was my wedding gown, which I could see hanging in the adjacent room.

"Is this some kind of prank?"

Chris Stevens shook his head but didn't look me in the eye. Was I supposed to be thankful he'd taken the time to tell me all of this in person? Or was I supposed to wish he would get out of my sight? The answer was up in the air.

"The least you can do is tell me why." There was plenty more he could do, but all I wanted to know right now was why. Why had he waited so long to say anything? Why didn't he just call everything off months ago?

Chris sighed and raked his fingers through his hair. "I'm not ready to get married, and I'm sorry it took me this long to realize it. And then to tell you."

Although he was still talking, I had tuned him out. I could hear the underlying 'but' in his statement and thought about questioning him further. Was I prepared for the answer he might give? Not that I hadn't had my share of doubts leading up to the big day, because marriage was a gigantic step. Things hadn't been fantastic between us lately, but I chalked it up to all the stress that was going into planning such an enormous affair. Plus, he'd acted normal at our rehearsal dinner the night before.

Another question roared to the surface as I tried to get my emotions in order. Hurt and anger topped the list, but I wanted to do my best to remain calm. In this case, throwing a scene—no matter how much I wanted to—wouldn't make the situation any better. But I needed to know the answer. "Is there someone else?"

"No, of course not. Did you think that I would stoop that low?"

"Well, given the situation at hand, I—"

The front door to the hotel suite opening cut off my words. Out of the corner of my eye, I saw my sister come into the room. Although I had some other close friends, both Chris and I had decided to keep our bridal party small, with just his best friend standing beside him and my sister standing beside me. That way, we thought, would make things less complicated, and I couldn't have been more right, given where things stood at this moment.

"Hey, you aren't supposed to see the bride until you do your first look photos." Although my sister's voice had a teasing lilt to it, the signs of annoyance were on her face. It was clear she wasn't a big fan of Chris' presence where I was getting ready. I mean, where I had been getting ready.

"It's funny you should say that, because we aren't getting married." My gaze shifted in intensity as my eyes moved from staring down Chris to looking at Angie. There was no way I was going to cry over this situation in front of them. What I was going to do was take control. "We are calling the wedding off." I turned my attention back to Chris and said, "You should be the one to go downstairs and tell our families you didn't want to do this, and that the wedding is off. But give me an hour before you do."

He nodded his head. "Fair enough. To be honest, you're taking this way better than I thought you would."

I shrugged. "I mean, what else can I do? This is for the best, and I also wish you the best. Please leave my room."

Chris hesitated for a moment before exiting.

Angie rushed over to me and threw her arms around me. "Did all that just happen?"

"I think it did. And I haven't had time to think about it, so before it gets to me, I need you to help me with something."

"Anything."

"I need you to book me another room at another hotel." I examined the drink that Chris had given me just before he'd told me he didn't want to get married. One sniff confirmed he had brought me hot green tea, a drink that I couldn't stand.

---

WHEN ANGIE SAID she would do anything, she stuck true to her word. She made sure that I got out of my old hotel room as quickly as possible and even checked me out, so I didn't have to face any questions from the front desk or from any guests who might have been lingering around the main floor of the hotel. Then again, I had full and utter confidence in her because not only was she my sister, but she also worked as my assistant. I didn't know where I would be without her.

I was safely at another hotel about fifteen minutes away from the venue where I was supposed to become Mrs. Stevens. Only one person in the world knew where I was. I asked Angie not to tell anyone, including our parents, where I had gone. I checked my phone once more and saw my mom had responded to a text message I'd sent a few minutes ago. I typed a message letting her know I was okay and just needed time alone. I knew she wanted to help me out with this, but I needed a moment to myself.

I placed my cell phone face down on the bathroom countertop so I wouldn't get distracted by any notifications. I had debated on turning off my phone but figured it was best to leave it on, just in case there was an emergency. I looked at myself in the mirror and wanted to cry at the reflection staring back at me. Even though I had put on a brave face in front of Chris and

Angie, I was heartbroken. What I couldn't determine was the source of my heartbreak. Was it over the demise of a relationship? Or was it what lay ahead in the unknown? Having a small amount of time to reflect on what had happened, I could see why he'd called it off—and it had nothing to do with wedding planning. We didn't have as much of a connection over the last few months, and the smaller arguments we had, had been kicked up a notch. But once again, I had pegged it as being a part of the stress over the wedding and thought things would get better after the wedding. Chris had had different feelings and was brave enough to pull the trigger before we'd made it legal.

I grabbed my comb and slowly combed out the curls which would have been a part of my wedding hairdo before throwing my hair into a ponytail. I took out my make-up remover wipes and went to town on the rest of my wedding day look. It took me longer than usual, because my make-up artist had made sure it wouldn't melt during the wedding.

It took quite a few wipes and washing my face to put the last nail in the coffin of my wedding day look. I snatched my phone off the countertop, and as I was walking into the living area, there was a knock on the door. My heart skipped a beat as I peeped out of the small hole above the instructions directing guests on where to go in case of an emergency. I rolled my eyes at myself before I opened the door and greeted the person with a polite smile. During the time it had taken me to get situated in my room, I forgot that I had ordered a lot of food for myself and Angie, who had run back to our old hotel to wrap up some last-minute things before she came to stay in the suite that adjoined mine.

Once I scribbled my name on the receipt and paid the tip, I let out a breath I hadn't known I was holding. I looked at the feast presented before me and sent a quick text to Angie, letting her know our food and wine were here. As I threw my phone on my bed, there was another knock on the door. I looked through the peephole once more and opened it to find Angie standing on the other side.

"I just sent you a text."

"I saw but figured it was easier to just knock on the door." She looked at the food. "This looks great."

"I know, right?" I glanced down at the food and let out a quick breath when my eyes landed on my sister. "Thanks for everything."

Angie stared at me with one eyebrow raised. "For what? You paid for all of this. Which again, I have to remind you, it pays to be a romance author."

I chuckled. She wasn't wrong. I'd been fortunate enough to make a full-time living off of my work as a romance writer. Having the ability to create characters and worlds that other people enjoyed was something I'd fallen into and loved. Plus, it gave me the ability to research different places and travel to different locations to gain inspiration and information for my books.

"Yeah, but I'm a romance author who can't write or have their own happy ending."

My words caused Angie to look at me, and I could see the pity in her eyes for a flash of a second before she could mask her feelings. She then turned away from me and headed over to the items that had been delivered to our room just moments ago. Angie turned back to me, wine in hand, and said, "Crap, this bottle has to be opened with a corkscrew."

The dry chuckle that fell from my lips while Angie mumbled some choice words, caused a small smile to appear on her face. Opening wine bottles with a corkscrew had always given her trouble, and she probably assumed now would be no exception. I walked over to the kitchen area and pulled open the drawers in search of a corkscrew. I found it in the last one, and I walked over to help my sister conquer this latest conquest.

She eagerly handed me the bottle, and within about a minute, we were both sipping on a glass of pinot noir and munching on our french fries and hamburgers, while the television played in the background.

"How are you taking everything that's happening?" Her sudden words led me to stop chewing while I debated in my head how to respond to the question.

"I feel a multitude of emotions, and I'm sure some of them I haven't been able to grasp yet."

"Well, do you want to talk about all of this?"

"Kind of? I can't imagine how much this is going to cost to cancel everything, especially the day of the wedding. I wonder if I could send Chris a bill for the things I paid for out of pocket."

"At least there won't be much to separate in terms of housing and money yet."

I nod my head. "Good point. We hadn't even had much time to co-mingle our things before today, anyway." Chris and I had moved in together about a month ago. Well, I had moved into his apartment, and the idea was that we were going to add my name on the lease and complete most of the paperwork after the wedding. Guess I didn't have to worry about that either. I slapped my hand on my forehead. "Well, shit, I guess I need to find a new apartment too."

"You can move in with me until you get on your feet. The rest of the things you won't need right away can be placed into storage."

I turned to my sister with tears in my eyes. Although I had stopped the tears from falling when I was wiping off my makeup, I couldn't this time. "Thanks, I truly appreciate it, but I don't want to cramp your style either. I could probably move back home until I figure something else out."

"Is that something you want to do?" She had a point. Living at home with Mom and Dad had been okay when I was a teenager, but what would it be like as an adult? "I'll sleep on it tonight and decide tomorrow. I need to make arrangements to get my things out of Chris's place as soon as possible. Which is going to be a pain in the ass, since I just moved in there."

"Don't worry about it right now. Whatever you need, I'm sure Mom, Dad, and I will help as much as we can. For now, we can relax, and then you can figure out what you want to do from there.

TWO

BARRETT

**Present Day**

"PIERCE. Come to my office in five."

My boss's call ended with a resounding slam that would have made me jump if I hadn't been expecting it. I had been waiting for his call because I already knew what this conversation was going to be about. In fact, it surprised me it had taken him this long.

In all the years I had worked at Parker and Gold, an investment banking firm in New York City, I had never been on the receiving end of Gary's wrath. About two years ago, I had been promoted to Vice President, and my job mostly focused on managing the client relations within my portfolio. That's what I assumed had gotten me into hot water right now.

I threw on my suit jacket I had haphazardly thrown over one of the extra chairs in my office. While I straightened my jacket, I looked outside and noticed the weather had slowly become gray as the day went on, mentally trying to remember if I still had my spare umbrella in the office. I took a deep breath and walked out my office door and down the hall to hear what Gary had to say. I waved at his receptionist, Lizzy, and the look she gave me confirmed Gary was on a tear. Although I had an idea what it was about, it shouldn't have been enough to get him this angry.

Gary told me to come in within a second of me knocking on his door. I entered the room and closed the door, determined not to show any inclination into what I might be thinking. Gary was busy scribbling on a piece of paper and didn't acknowledge my presence. I could tell by his beet red appearance that he was pissed. His new complexion made its way up to and past his balding head. I knew he was trying to intimidate me by making me wait, but I couldn't care less.

The scribbling continued for a minute or two based on the clock on Gary's wall. He put the pen down and finally looked up at me. "Have a seat." He gestured to the chairs in front of his desk, a mirror of the ones in my office. I sat and was ready to meet my fate.

"Pierce, when was the last time you took a vacation?"

If he was trying to throw me off kilter, he had succeeded. I was expecting him to yell and carry on, and this was the exact opposite. "Um, before I came to work here?"

"You've been here for five years, right?"

I thought for a moment and nodded. "That's about right."

"And you haven't taken a vacation day."

"Nope. Haven't felt a need to. I enjoy working for Parker and Gold."

"And I appreciate your dedication, I do. But you need a break."

"Is this because of the Taylor account?" I asked with a sigh. "He changed his mind last minute and—"

"I understand what happened there. But you fumbled part of the Clark account as well."

"I can explain that—"

Gary brushed a hand across his forehead before looking me in the eyes. "Pierce, take a vacation. Recharge. Have some fun. Your performance is suffering, and it worries us that you might burn out. You are one of the best, and we want to keep it that way. Usually you don't make mistakes like you've done on these."

I sat back in the chair and thought about what he'd said. He was right; I rarely made mistakes. Although these had been small ones, and I had owned up to them, it still wasn't acceptable. I glanced out of the window to the right of Gary and said to no one in particular, "I guess you're right."

I left his office and headed back to my own. Just as I was about to sit down, there was a knock on my door.

"Come in."

My co-worker, Colin, stuck his head around the door. "Everything cool? Heard Gary was angry."

"Yep. In fact, the meeting didn't go as bad as I thought it would."

Colin eased his way into my office and shut the door. "How bad was it?"

I leaned back in my chair. "We both knew the couple of mistakes that had happened recently were going to get brought up."

"Right."

"They did, but he kind of brushed over them. Mentioned I should look at going on vacation."

"Wait. He recommended you go on vacation? You're kidding."

I shook my head.

"Sometimes, I swear you are the luckiest SOB... people have gotten reprimanded for less."

"I know. But I'll take his suggestion. Looks like I'm going on vacation."

———

"YOU'RE GOING ON VACATION? Really? I've been saying you should take one for years. Years! Where are you going?"

The high pitched shrill that my mother's voice took on in excitement forced me to close my eyes and cover the ear closest to the phone. "I'm headed to the Poconos for some much-needed relaxation, according to my boss." I tossed another sweater into my suitcase.

"Have you gone on vacation since you graduated from Wharton?"

I stop moving for a second before replying, "Yes, I went to Aruba with a couple of buddies from high school."

"I forgot about that," mumbled my mother before clearing her throat. "Have you been on one since that trip? Are they going with you this time?"

I sighed. "No." Both of my buddies from high school now were married with families of their own. It would be way harder for them to skip town on such short notice.

"I knew it, and it's about time then. I hate to see you being so overworked. You need to take time out for yourself sometimes."

I dropped a pair of jeans into my suitcase and then rubbed my hands over my face. I knew she was right, but I didn't have to like the fact she was right. "I know, Mom. It's something you mention just about every time we talk on the phone."

"I'm only looking out for you."

Those words brought a small smile to my face. "I know. I'm kind of excited to be going to be honest."

"Oh, really? Why is that?"

"Not having to wear a suit for a bit will be a nice change in wardrobe." Although I loved my job, wearing suits day in and day out could get tiring. It shocked me that I was able to find anything besides suits and gym clothes in my wardrobe to put into my suitcase. Had it really been that long since I had seen those other clothes in my closet?

"I'm sure it will be. Where are you staying in the Poconos?"

"I'm staying at the Holiday Springs Resort. It is a five-star property that has cottages, cabins, and hotel rooms guests can stay in. I chose to stay in a hotel room to be closer to the restaurant and bar in the main lodge."

My mom laughed. "Why does that not surprise me? I know you too well."

"That you do. Listen, Mom, I need to finish packing, so I'll let you go."

"Sounds good. Have a safe trip."

"Thanks, bye."

I had just finished putting another pair of jeans into my suitcase when my stomach growled, reminding me how I hadn't eaten in a while. I headed into the kitchen to see what I might be able to throw together. As I riffled through the cupboards, I realized how infrequently I had been home. I started tossing out-of-date items from my refrigerator into the garbage—most had gone bad—as I tried to think of where I could order food. Figuring since I was already clearing out my fridge, it made sense to clean out my freezer too. Before starting that task, I put in an order to my favorite pizzeria. By the time I had finished, my pizza had arrived, and while I ate in silence, I picked up the brochure from Holiday Springs Gary's wife had emailed him before our conversation.

I skimmed the front cover before turning the page, hoping to get a quick idea of what I could do to occupy my time at the resort. Seeing nothing that was really pulling my interest, I hoped that this forced vacation wouldn't be a complete waste of time.

I flipped through the brochure again, paying closer attention, but still nothing caught my eye. I knew there had to be more to this place than the brochure was letting on, so I walked into my office and grabbed my computer. It took only a few seconds before I found the Holiday Springs Resort website. I browsed through some attractions on the resort's property and off. I couldn't help but chuckle when I saw one of the local bars in town was named the Drunken Yeti and quickly put it down on my must visit list. I also added hiking one of the trails near the resort if the weather allowed. I couldn't remember the last time I had exercised outside, let alone had gone hiking, so that would be a change to my usual routine. Skiing was also on the table as well as the cooking class, but I thought I'd feel a little awkward doing that one alone.

Feeling satisfied with what I had discovered about the resort, I closed my laptop and went back to packing for the trip.

## THREE

## NICOLE

I stepped out of my car and looked at the entrance to the Holiday Springs Resort. Luckily, I had gotten a parking spot close to the entrance, which meant it was less of a trek for me to get to the front doors. The crunching of the snow under my boots and a car in the distance were all I heard as I made my way toward the large stone pillars encompassing the doorway that would lead to the start of my vacation. Once I reached the stairs, I stopped to look up and noticed the metal sign over the doorway that read Holiday Springs. It brought a lightness to my heart after dealing with the end of my relationship several months prior. Still I wondered if I had made the right decision booking this trip at all, let alone between Christmas and New Year's Day.

I trudged along and made my way into the main lodge, peering around to figure out where I was going next. The main lodge was made of all wood and thankfully, it took no time for me to find the front desk. It was simply decorated with holiday lights and garland with a big Christmas tree in one corner. I could tell they were putting in the effort to show some holiday cheer while not trying to overdo it at the same time. I focused my attention back to the front desk, and that was when I noticed it, too, had some holiday decorations across it as well. There was already a man being helped by someone, so I stood back and waited my turn. That turn came quickly when a woman walked out from what I assumed was a staff room and gave me a bright smile.

"Hello, how may I help you?"

"Hi, Cassie," I said as I read the name that was printed on her name tag. "I'm checking in this afternoon. My name is Nicole Ford."

Cassie's fingers moved across the keyboard with ease before she looked up at me. "Mrs. Stevens, it looks like everything is set for you. All you have to do is sign here and here, which says you understand our rules and regulations and will pay for any incidentals, should they occur."

I felt my head jolt back involuntarily. Some of the feelings I thought I had repressed sprang to the surface. I had done my best to avoid that last name over the last few months and hearing it again had taken me by surprise, even though it was partially the reason I was here.

"It's Ms. Ford," I said, as I tried to make sure my voice was as level as possible. If this had been right after we cancelled the wedding, I was sure I would have burst into tears. Thankfully, Holiday Springs Resort had allowed me to push my arrival date out by several months, giving me some time to wrap my head around the situation and my feelings. Cassie looked at me before she squinted at the computer screen and looked back at me.

"Oh, I am so sorry! I should have looked closer at the notes listed on your file, but you were listed under your married name and in one of our cabins we use for couples who are honeymooning with us, and I—" A blush appeared on her cheeks as she gathered her blonde curls and threw them over one shoulder. I tried to give a polite smile, hoping to diffuse some of the awkwardness of the situation.

"Well, I, for one, think that you look more like a Ford than a Stevens, anyway."

The new addition to our conversation made me swivel my head toward the unfamiliar voice. The man who had been standing at the front desk before I arrived had turned his attention toward my situation. I stared at him for a moment and hadn't realized I was holding my breath until it all came rushing out of me at once. Not only had his deep baritone voice caught me off guard, but so had his crystal blue eyes. His dark hair was perfectly styled yet had taken on a look like he had just stepped out of bed. His broad shoulders filled out the white cable sweater, and his dark-colored jeans and brown boots were straight out of a catalogue advertising clothing for your next winter getaway.

"Thank you?" I asked, more curious about the intrusion than hearing more about his opinion of my last name. The smile he sent me before angling towards me sent a small chill through my body, although I could have chalked it up to it being the dead of winter. I shook the thoughts of how there was no way I could be cold with my heavy winter coat on, in a building which had the heat on and a fire roaring in a fireplace surrounded by a large stone mantel. It had been hard to miss when I'd walked into the room.

"No problem, Ms. Ford." The man's gaze burned a hole straight through me. Based on his looks alone, he had caused me to think thoughts I hadn't envisioned in quite some time. He grabbed his suitcase, the keys to his hotel room, and his coat, which he had laid across the suitcase.

Before he could turn around and walk away, I cleared my throat and asked, "And what is your last name?"

His gaze landed back on me. "It's Pierce. I'm sure I'll see

you around." With that, he gave me a smile I wanted to read more into and went on his way through the lodge.

"Ms. Ford?"

I turned back to Cassie, who gave me a tentative smile.

"I'm sorry once again. Here are the keys, a map, and a welcome folder. It includes all the activities you can do here and restaurants in the resort and nearby in town."

"Thanks a lot, and don't worry about calling me the wrong last name earlier. It was an honest mistake." I placed the items Cassie had given me into my tote bag and made my way back out to the front of the main lodge. When I walked down the stairs, a powerful gust of wind reminded me it was December and I was in the mountains. The holiday cheer was still alive at the resort as we were getting closer to New Year's Day.

I smiled at a woman walking by as I headed back toward my car. When I reached my red sedan, I opened the door and flung myself into the driver's seat. After placing my purse on the passenger's seat, I studied the map before backing out of the parking space I had so recently entered.

Thankfully, the map Cassie had given me was straightforward, and I soon pulled up to Cabin 6 and parked in the parking spot designated for me. When I exited my car, I stared at the cabin in wonder. This was supposed to be the honeymoon my ex-fiancé and I took that would have been his dream vacation. No work and no stress had been the things he said when we were looking up locations we potentially wanted to go to. Yet here I was, alone, staring at this cabin meant to be filled with love, joy, and lots and lots of sex.

Another gust of wind reminded me I was standing outside of my car and staring at a building, so I needed to get a move on it. I bent over and placed the map back inside my tote bag along with some other things I'd left in my center console. I grabbed the tote bag and circled to the trunk of my car, hitting the button on remote to unlock it as I went. I unloaded my two suitcases and headed up to my 'romantic' getaway.

"This is not too bad at all," I whispered to myself after I opened the front door and looked over the threshold. Just from the little I could see, the website had not been kidding about this being a luxurious, romantic getaway. The suite included a king-size bed with crisp white linens and a small sitting area with a flat screen TV hanging over a fireplace just a few feet away. Before checking out the rest of the room, I pulled my suitcases inside and closed the door. Leaving them where they were, I gave myself a quick tour of my home away from home and was happy to see not only were the bedroom and the living room area stunning, so was the bathroom. The bathroom included a beautiful white soaking tub and a large shower with tiles that looked like they were made of marble.

I stood still for a second and remembered Angie wanted me to text her when I arrived. I fired off a text message to her and wasn't surprised when she called me back in return.

"I'm glad you made it there safely. How is it?"

"The property is stunning." I told her about what I had seen so far, including my room. "And check-in was mostly a breeze."

"What do you mean?"

"While I was being checked in, the person who was handling it made a mistake and called me Mrs. Stevens."

"Oh, no. I made sure to tell the resort you were to be called Ms. Ford."

"Oh, yeah, I know, and the woman quickly corrected herself and apologized, but it still stung a little. I'm pretty much over it now." I paused for a moment, debating whether or not I should tell Angie this part of the story. Figuring I had nothing to lose, I continued talking. "Especially because it led to me meeting a man who was also checking in at the front desk."

"Oh, really? Tell me more."

"Now I don't know how long he's gonna stay here, nor do I know where he is staying on the property, because that would be a little too creepy even for my nosy ass."

"Wait, what information did you find out?"

"Well, I do know his last name is Pierce."

"Is that it?" The way she said it made me think she thought I had done a pretty pathetic job of gathering information. She wasn't wrong, but I had also been thrown off my flirting game by the interaction with Cassie and was a bit rusty at it now anyway.

"Yep. But I would assume chances are, I'll see him around. At the very least, I assume he'll need to eat at some point, so maybe it'll be during mealtimes or something. The resort is big but not that big." I paused for a moment. "But, for crying out loud, I don't even know if he's dating someone or married."

"Well, could you tell if he was there with anyone else?"

"As far as I could see, no, and I didn't notice a ring on his finger when he picked up his coat. But that also doesn't mean anything." I smashed my phone between my ear and my shoulder and tightened the ponytail I had thrown my hair in before I'd left my newish apartment. "But I have to admit, he was smoking hot."

"Well, just see what happens. I mean, you're single for the first time in several years and he might be too. If you see him around, doesn't hurt to start up a conversation with him."

I sighed. "You know how much I hate to admit that you're right."

"I know. And don't you ever forget it. I have to go, but I'll call you tomorrow. Does tomorrow morning still work for us to chat on the phone?" Before I left, Angie had mentioned wanting to talk over the phone more, since I wouldn't be there in person, and I needed to get this book done as soon as possible, and I agreed.

"Sure. Sounds good."

"Have a great rest of the day and don't do anything I wouldn't do."

"You're hilarious. Bye." I hung up the phone and took another look around the space.

Although this hadn't been my number one choice for a honeymoon destination, maybe coming here for vacation anyway wouldn't be so bad after all.

## FOUR

BARRETT

I drummed my fingers against my knee as I debated whether to check up on work. It wouldn't hurt to take a look at a couple of emails while I waited for the whiskey I ordered. I glanced at my phone again before looking up at the television. On it was a quick rundown of the latest news regarding the sports world, and it made me try to think back to the last time I'd even attended a sporting event. Maybe it was a New York Giants game in one of their executive suites during their playoff run a few years ago? That whole evening had been spent networking and talking to potential clients versus taking the time to enjoy the football game taking place in front of me.

After the announcers went through the top five sports stories of the day, I glanced down at the space in front of me, realizing that Jeremy, the bartender, hadn't given me my whiskey yet. I looked over and saw him chatting with a woman. I heard her chuckle at something Jeremy said, and she looked over her shoulder, her eyes meeting mine. It was the woman I'd encountered at the front desk earlier. I had thought she was cute when we met, but right now, she was downright stunning. Her hair, which had been up in a ponytail this morning, now fell in cascading waves just past her shoulders. Her red sweater and denim jeans hugged her curves, but her smile was what caused me to stop breathing for a second. She had looked stressed after being called the wrong last name, but now she looked happier and relaxed.

"Pierce," she said as she walked over to my stool in front of the bar at the Bear Claw Lounge.

"Ford," I replied in return. And just like that, the whiskey I had ordered appeared in front of me. "But we can go by first names. I'm Barrett."

"Nicole. It's nice to meet you."

"Great to meet you. Would you like to have a seat? I'm happy to buy a round."

Nicole hesitated for a moment before sitting on the stool and asking Jeremy for a menu. He handed her one, and Nicole smiled at me before turning to Jeremy. "Can I have the mojito?"

Jeremy nodded. "Coming right up." He hurried away to make Nicole's drink. I bet he'd have her drink to her in no time.

"Why did you decide to come to Holiday Springs?" I couldn't think of anything better to say than that? Normally I didn't take too much stock into how I said something, because I never had a problem finding the right words or getting tongue tied. This was a new feeling.

Nicole took a deep breath before she said, "A few months ago, the plan was for me to come here on my honeymoon, but that didn't happen because my ex-fiancé decided he didn't want to get married just a few hours before our wedding. So, it took me a few months to get myself together enough to even broach the idea of what I should do about the honeymoon. I decided to hell with it; I still should be able to take the honeymoon I was supposed to be going on. Although Holiday Springs was where he wanted to go, he didn't protest me taking a trip instead, so that's what I did. And so far, I'm not regretting that decision."

Nicole paused for a moment before she placed a hand on my shoulder. "Sorry to unload all of that on you when we just met."

Her touch jumpstarted my pulse and caused my heart to beat a tick faster. It took me a minute to find the words to say, but the words that fell out of my mouth felt inadequate. "Don't worry about it. After all, I asked the question." Once again, that was the best I could come up with? I took a swig of my whiskey. As I was placing my glass down on the bar table top, Jeremy arrived with Nicole's mojito and placed it in front of her.

"Let me know if you need anything else." The smirk he gave Nicole told me he was mostly talking to her, but he spared a glance at me before making his way down to the other end of the bar to attend to other patrons.

Nicole took a dainty sip from her drink before closing her eyes for a moment and then turning her attention back to me. "This is delicious. Thank you." She paused again before continuing. "Why are you here? Wait, that came out way harsher than I meant."

"No harm, no foul. I am here because I was forced to take a vacation." A light chuckle left her luscious lips, which drew my attention to them. Images exploring them with my own filtered into my mind.

"Do you have a thing against vacations? Why were you forced to take one?"

I debated how I was going to answer the question as I stared at my drink. "It's a bit of a long story."

Nicole took a larger sip from her drink. "I don't know about you, but I don't have anywhere to be. So, lay it on me." There was nothing I could do to control the smirk on my face, and I saw when the realization of what she had said reached hers. The light blush blooming on her cheeks before she threw her hands to her face was endearing. "I didn't mean it like that."

I waved her off. "Don't worry about it. I knew what you

meant. My boss thought it was a good idea for me to take a vacation."

Nicole's head shot back, and she raised an eyebrow. "What boss would want you to take a vacation?"

"One who sees that your job performance has gone down and is trying to save you from yourself. Then again, I haven't taken a vacation since I started working my current job, and I've been there for five years."

Nicole said nothing, but her lips made the shape of an O. That drew my attention back to them, and the dirty thoughts from earlier swam back to the forefront of my brain.

"Sometimes it's hard for me to tell myself to take a vacation given that I'm my own boss, but at least I've taken a vacation within the last few years. You need the rest, even if you're staying at home, at least that's my philosophy."

I nodded and took a mouthful of my whiskey. Once the liquid cleared my throat, I asked, "What is it that you do?"

Nicole gently swirled her drink in her glass but didn't respond right away. I couldn't read her expression. I waited a beat before I was about to say something to keep the conversation going, but she spoke first.

"I'm an author. I write romance novels and—" She stopped mid-sentence and glanced down at her drink.

"You what?"

"It's just that usually when I tell people that I write romance novels for a living, I can feel their judgement. It's something I've gotten used to, so my initial reaction is to wait for someone to say something slick about my profession."

"Do you like what you do?" I saw by her expression that my question took her by surprise.

"Hell yeah, I do. I get the opportunity to entertain people all over the world with my words. Few people can say that they can do the same." She picked up her glass. "That's a brilliant point, thanks for reminding me of that."

"If you need me to remind you about it again, let me know. I'm here."

Nicole glanced at me over her glass, and I couldn't stop the smirk I sent her way.

The look on my face made her laugh, and that was when I noticed the dimple in one of her cheeks. Her eyes lit up like the Rockefeller Center Christmas tree. I was happy she seemed to be enjoying my company as much as I was enjoying hers.

"If you had the option to do anything else for the rest of your life, what would you do?

"Is this a version of the 'where do you see yourself in five years' question?"

"Maybe?"

Nicole laughed. "Although I do love writing romance novels, and it is my dream job, I would start some sort of program that would encourage children who want to write. I know some kids aren't as fortunate, and I want to give at least some of them the opportunity to explore their dreams."

Her answer wasn't one I was expecting. In a world that tended to be selfish, her wanting to help others was refreshing and spoke to what I imagined was her character as a person.

"How about you?"

I rubbed a hand across the stubble on my chin as my brain tried to come up with an answer. "My thoughts usually revolve around work, so I don't know what I'd be doing, if I'm being honest."

Nicole smiled and gently nudged me with her foot. "You can think of something. Come on."

"If I could do anything else, I'd probably do something with fitness. I think exercising is important, and I try to take time out to do it multiple times a week. I'm going to try to get into the gym while I'm here, since I won't have to worry about working long hours."

"Hopefully you won't spend your entire vacation just focusing on working out."

"A distraction would be nice."

I knew she understood the meaning of my words by the light blush that reappeared on her cheeks. I felt this magnetism toward her that I couldn't quite explain, especially since we had just met. The smile that played on her lips made me wonder if she felt the same. The only reason I knew about it was because I couldn't remove my eyes from her, trying to take in every detail, because I knew this night would end way too soon.

"Is there anything you'd love to do while you're here?"

I shook my head. "I've looked over the list of activities a few times, and I'm open to just about anything. I'm pretty happy just hanging around and relaxing in a bar, much like this one. How about you? Is there something you want to do while here?"

"I've been dying to go ice skating again." I didn't doubt her one bit based on how her face lit up as she said the words. "I haven't been since I was a little girl and would love to have that experience again."

I made a mental note to check when the rink was open before I could catch myself. If she wanted me to come along and for us to see each other again, I had no problem setting it up. It would be great to give her the opportunity to just enjoy herself after what I suspect had been a wild few months after her wedding had been cancelled.

We spent most of the night talking about everything and anything under the sun. Her ambition and the goals she set for herself when it came to running her own business intrigued me. I spent most of my time dealing with big corporations. Hearing about the actions that a small business owner was taking was a welcome reprieve from the number crunching I did on almost a daily basis.

I changed the subject. "Where are you from originally?"

She dabbed her lips with the napkin that had been in a canister next to some condiments across the bar. "I've moved around quite a bit, because my dad's job transferred him quite a few times over the years, but I've spent most of my childhood and adult life in Philly. How about you?"

"I'm a New Yorker. Born and raised."

That comment seemed to interest her, because she leaned forward and rested her chin on her fist. "I've been to New York several times. I've always wanted to live there." She stopped herself. "Wait."

She pulled away from the bar top and grabbed her purse that she had hung underneath the counter near her feet. She starting digging into it and quickly pulled out her phone. "I can't remember my schedule off the top of my head, but I think I'm going to be in New York in the next couple of months..." She muttered to herself, and she fiddled around with her phone, more than likely trying to find her calendar app.

"Ah, here it is. I swear I wouldn't know my head from my ass if it weren't for Angie sometimes." Her fingers continued to fly over her phone screen before giving me a pointed look, "She's my sis-assistant."

"Sister assistant?"

"She's my older sister, and I hired her as my assistant in the middle of last year. Has been helping me schedule my life and run my business ever since. One of the best decisions I'd ever made."

"Oh, okay."

"Yes. I'm going to be in New York City in March. I have a book signing I'm attending to support my new book."

"Ah, okay. March can be pretty hit or miss for the city in terms of weather." I thought about mentioning we should meet up if her trip ends up working out but didn't want to be too forward.

"Same with Philly... hey! If you want, we can get drinks or something while I'm in town."

"That sounds like a plan."

Her face lit up once more, and given my ability to analyze any situation to death, I realized she had been nervous about asking me.

We spent more time talking and getting to know each other and ordered one more drink and some glasses of water.

"We played a small prank on one of our friends. If I remember correctly, he was the first one of us to get his license and a car for his birthday. It was more of a rite of passage type thing, because since we were in the heart of the city, you really didn't need one. A few days after he got the car, we got saran wrap and wrapped his car in it."

"You guys did what?" Nicole exclaimed. "I didn't know where this was going, but I wasn't expecting that."

"He wasn't happy."

"Really? I couldn't ever imagine why he would have been pissed."

I smirked at her sarcasm. "You never would have thought you'd see some kids run so fast down the street. What made things worse is that he was on the track team, so honestly it was pretty silly to run away," I said, finishing up one of the stories I had offered to tell about some of the trouble my friends and I would get into while growing up in New York City. She let out a thunderous laugh, and I found the sound refreshing. In my life, it was rare to find someone who wouldn't try to mute their own joy in the presence of strangers, but the longer I talked to her, I realized Nicole was wearing her heart on her sleeve, which made it easier to learn what she liked and what she didn't.

"Hi. Sorry to interrupt, but we're about to close up."

I looked up and found Jeremy holding on to a piece of paper. He placed the receipt on the counter, equal distance between me and Nicole.

Nicole sat up in her chair and grabbed her phone, which had been face down on the table. She let out a gasp. "Oh, I didn't know it was so late. I need to head back to my cabin."

"I'm staying here, but how about I walk you to your car?"

She hesitated for a moment before nodding. Score. Before she could grab it, I swiped the receipt off the table. "Should I take this up to the cash register at the other end of the bar?"

"Now, Barrett, I can help pay—"

"No need."

"I can close out the tab," Jeremy said, and I handed my credit card to him. He dashed back to the cash register.

"You didn't have to do that." Nicole gathered her things and placed her purse on her shoulder.

"I know I didn't, but I wanted to." And I truly did.

She beamed at me, and I felt my heart race. What was it about this woman that drew me to her?

Once we reached the bar, Jeremy handed me back my credit card. "Thanks so much for joining us tonight." Both Nicole and I said our thanks and goodbyes as I finished giving a tip and signing the receipt.

We strolled outside, making small talk until we reached a small red sedan.

"This is me."

I didn't want this to be the end of the night, but I knew it had to be. I stood by her car for a second before an idea popped into my head. "If my mom were here, and I didn't ask you this, it would earn me a tap in the back of my head. Text me when you get back to your cabin, so I know that everything is all right."

"Is this your way of asking for my number?"

"No... well, I didn't think about it like that, but I guess it is. Is it all right if I could get your number?"

"Sure," said Nicole, and she rattled off the ten digits. I then called her so she had my phone number too. "You know, you could have just asked me for my number instead of coming up with that excuse."

"Oh, it wasn't an excuse. I wanted to make sure you were okay, given that you are going to be driving at night. It is something my mother ingrained in us, when we were younger growing up in New York City."

"Well, that makes sense." Nicole shuffled her feet, trying to decide what to do next. She leaned into me slightly and glanced at my lips. Taking a cue from her, I took a step forward. And my lips landed on hers. The kiss took on a mind of its own, and once we broke apart, it left us both breathless. Although we were out in the cold, my body felt like it was burning up and yearning for her lips to find mine once more.

"Is it okay if we see more of each other while we are here?" I looked down at her, and my gaze shifted between her dark brown eyes to the condensation each of our breaths made.

"After that kiss, I think that would be a fantastic idea."

This vacation might be fun after all.

## FIVE

## NICOLE

I woke up with a small smile on my face. My time with Barrett last night was the highlight of the last few months, and it had been the first time I had belly-laughed in a long time. It didn't hurt that I was very attracted to him, with his broad shoulders and sparkling blue eyes, which lit up when he was telling me a story about something that had happened to him. I was happy he mentioned we should see each other and had come up with the excuse to trade phone numbers.

I had texted him once I'd arrived at my cabin, and we sent messages to each other for most of the night until we fell asleep. Although it was just a series of text messages, the thrill of seeing whether or not there was a connection with another person was alive and well.

I made a small cup of coffee and glanced out my window, taking note of the sun shining through the cabin. Although it looked bright, I assumed it was still blistering cold out, given the time of year. I tried to get my mind right as I walked over to my desk in the cabin with my mug in hand. The smell of coffee was one of the best smells in the world to me, especially as I settled down to get some work done on my laptop. A noise from my phone interrupted my thoughts. I glanced down at the device and saw a notification that caused a pang in my chest.

**First draft due to editor in one month.**

It couldn't be a month out already. Then again, I had started this book before I had gotten thrown into the throes of wedding planning, so the news shouldn't have shocked me. Since I wasn't going to let that news ruin my mood, I placed my phone face down on the desk and turned my attention back to my computer. I threw my hair into a ponytail as I scanned the subject lines of the emails which remained unanswered in my inbox. The buzzing of my cell phone interrupted me once more. I took a quick glance down at the caller ID and saw it was sister calling me.

"Angie, hi." At first her call startled me because although we usually kept our communications to emails, texts or seeing each other in person, but then I remembered we had agreed to talk to each other over the phone this morning. What a nice change of pace.

"Hey! How's everything going at Holiday Springs?"

I thought of Barrett before I replied. "It's going pretty well. Is everything good with you?"

"Personally, yes, but there are some things I wanted to talk to you about regarding some of the work you have due."

"Okay. Lay it on me." I cringed as I wondered if I had forgotten something. I really needed to revisit using that phrase.

"Do you remember that *Romance Weekly* wanted to get an exclusive on your new release?"

Did. I. Remember? I had been waiting for *Romance Weekly* to get back to us for what felt like decades. *Romance Weekly* was one of the biggest magazines in the writing world for romance authors and being interviewed by them would be an honor. "Of course, I remember. A lot of things were up in the air because of my book."

"Well, they want to do an interview with you in a month, if that's possible. They are also hoping to receive an advance copy of your book."

Her words temporarily caused my heart rate to fall. I dropped down into a seated position on my bed and grabbed my chest. "They do?"

"Yes. They want, and I quote, 'the book that will be a guaranteed bestseller this year and the return of Nicole Ford.'"

"Lovely. Because I don't have a finished product to show at the moment. In fact, I didn't know if any of the words I wrote for this book were salvageable."

"Now, Nicole, I know you've had some pretty close calls over the years, but you don't have a handle on your manuscript? Like, at all?"

"Nope." I paused for a moment before I added, "Oh wait! I have something I was working on a couple of years ago I was hoping to revamp and make it a part of this book... but kind of scrapped because it didn't feel right."

Angie's quick intake of breath and deep breathing exercises told me she was doing everything to remain calm. But it wasn't going well.

"You know we have a huge PR campaign ready to go for this new book. Ads, blog interviews, and podcast appearances. Everyone is waiting for it."

My mind drifted back to Barrett. Visions of the way he raised his eyebrows when he was listening to me intently when I talked about my business. The way his sweater did zilch to hide the muscles underneath them. The way he talked passionately about his job, and the way he gently rubbed the back of my hand when I brought up some of the pain I'd experienced because of my cancelled wedding.

"I don't think I'll have a problem finishing my first draft quickly."

"Really?"

"Uh, huh. I think I'm shaking the fatigue I had because of everything that had happened with Chris. I should be able to find inspiration somewhere." Or under someone. And there went those dirty thoughts about Barrett. *You aren't on that level with him, so cool it.*

"Fantastic! I'll check in with you in about a few days, unless you want me to check in sooner? But also keep in mind that you are supposed to be on vacation."

"I know, I know, but this needs to get done. And this was supposed to be somewhat of a working vacation, anyway. If I need anything, I'll contact you and vice versa."

"I'll send a calendar invite over. I need to wrap up a few things on my end for you, but I will call you back so we can chat about how things are going... personally."

I rolled my eyes as I caught the double meaning behind her words. "Okay, Angie. I'll talk to you soon."

"Bye."

I still couldn't get Barrett out of mind, even while thinking about work. Thinking about him on the one hand made me happy, but on the other hand, I needed to stop. I had just met the man. That didn't stop me from envisioning some of the extracurricular activities we could do privately while at Holiday Springs, which would have been a fantastic way to spend part of the holiday season. But there was no way I would be jumping back into a relationship with anyone anytime soon. And this was only going on under the assumption that this was something he would want to do too.

My eyes danced across the room and landed on the device which had been my arch nemesis for the last few months. I strolled over to my computer and logged back into my laptop.

Once I had my word processing document open, the fact there was a blank screen staring back at me was upsetting. But what did I expect? That words would magically appear on the page?

And that started the cycle of me trying to force myself to write, but I couldn't. Then I would get annoyed with the fact that I couldn't. I opened up the two documents I was hoping to merge together to form the background of the story I wanted to write and then read through them. But I was still getting nowhere fast. A pinging noise came from my cell phone and stopped my thoughts in their tracks. I assumed it was Angie texting me about something else, but was surprised to find a message from Barrett.

**Barrett:** *How's everything going?*

**Me:** *Not as well as I would have hoped. I'm suffering from writer's block.*

**Barrett:** *Could I entice you to do something else? Maybe it will help with the writer's block.*

At this point, I'd do anything to move past it. And who knew? Maybe spending more time with him would inspire me to sit down and work on this book.

**Me:** *What did you have in mind?*

**Barrett:** *Well, I was reaching out to ask if you want to go ice skating. You'd mentioned how you used to go when you were younger.*

He remembered how much I loved ice skating? I couldn't stop the smile from appearing on my face. I hadn't been ice skating since I was a little girl, and it made me giddy inside. The feeling of the wind through my hair as I glided across the ice always made me happy. We used to go pretty regularly during the winter when I was a child, but had slowly stopped when I had gotten older. I didn't have anything to lose.

**Me:** *Let's do it. How long will it take you to get to the rink?*

**Barrett:** *Maybe 15 minutes?*
**Me:** *How about I meet you there in 30?*
**Barrett:** *Sounds good.*

## SIX

## BARRETT

"You sure the last time you ice skated was when you were a little girl?"

Nicole nodded. If she would have told me she'd been skating all her life, I would have believed her. She moved so effortlessly across the ice, almost like a swan on a lake. Now I didn't look too bad on the ice myself, and I had admitted to her I hadn't been ice skating in a long time either. But the way she skated reminded me of a ballerina with the American Ballet Theatre.

Her joyous giggles made me laugh as we made our way around the rink, ice skating around some other vacationers and locals at the resort. The way she slid her hand into mine while we skated lifted my spirit higher than getting praise for the good job I was doing at work.

Nicole let go of my hand and twirled around in a circle, and I couldn't resist teasing her. "Oh, now you're just showing off."

She stuck her tongue out at me. "Nope. Just proving to myself that I still have it."

I shook my head as she let out a hearty laugh once more. Her glossy, dark brown strands created almost a cape behind her as she swung around the rink. I wondered what it would look like spread across my bed—

"I'm getting a little tired. You would have never heard me say that years ago."

I chuckled, and we both slowed down but continued moving closer to the wall in hopes to avoid causing an accident. "I'm in the mood for some hot chocolate. Do you want any?" I didn't expect those words to come out of my mouth, because along with ice skating, I hadn't had hot chocolate in a long time, but I knew I didn't want to leave her side.

"Hot chocolate sounds amazing." I smiled at the emphasis she put on the word *amazing*. "Should we just head back to the resort to get it?"

"Sounds like a plan," I said.

We both went around the rink once more, her hand in mine, and when we came up to the exit, I helped her off the ice first before following suit. She and I went into the locker room to change back into our boots. Once we got all that sorted, we headed back and ended up in Bear Claw Lounge once more. We were seated at a table in the lounge, and thankfully, the bar had no problem fulfilling our desire for hot chocolate, and even asked if we wanted to have it spiked.

"You know, I think right now I just want straight hot chocolate with whipped cream. Unless you want to have a little something extra in yours."

"Nope, that works for me." I turned my attention to the server. "We'd like just the regular hot chocolate." The server headed back towards the bar with a polite smile.

"I can't believe we just went ice skating!" she exclaimed as she took off her bulky winter coat. The lights from the room danced in her eyes as she continued to experience the high which came from something she loved doing. "I don't even know what else to say."

"Oh, an author who can't find the right words to say? That must mean I did something right." I followed her lead and placed my coat behind my chair.

She made a big dramatic show of hitting my hand, but she only tapped it. "Hey, I'm on vacation and have writer's block. The words aren't flowing as easily. But I guess I can best describe it as being a childlike fun, if that makes sense."

I chuckled at a comment. "No, I think I understand what you're trying to say. Like, it's a very gleeful type of fun, a magical experience."

"Yes, like when someone goes to Disney World. The type of magic and atmosphere that the organization and the employees spend time building. It doesn't help that we are here right around the holidays, and the weather here is doing its part, with the snow on the ground and chill in the air. Thank you so much for suggesting this."

"Not a problem. I know we're just getting to know each other, so I thought this would be a great opportunity for us to learn more about each other."

"I would say you knocked it out of the park." I didn't realize how much was hedging on whether or not she liked the activity that I chose, but the way she beamed at me made me feel like I had just helped complete a major merger between two companies. Our server interrupted us when she brought our hot chocolate back to the table. We both thanked the woman, and Nicole held up her cup while staring at me. I tilted my head to the side and copied what she did.

"I thought we could cheer to something."

"Like what?"

"To more fun and exciting times at Holiday Springs Resort."

"I could agree to that. Cheers."

Our mugs clinked together, and we both took careful sips of the hot chocolate. I ended up with whipped cream on my upper lip, which must have been a hilarious sight to her, because she snorted and a smirk appeared on her face. "I'm so sorry. It's so rude of me to laugh at someone else."

"Oh, so you were laughing at me. Here I thought you might have been laughing with me. Yeah, that's rude," I said before taking my tongue and running it along my upper lip.

The smirk that had made a home on her lips slipped from her face, and a heated look in her eyes with her mouth slightly open took its place. Although the look only lasted for two seconds at most before she went back to her hot chocolate, I had caught it. There was a chance she was thinking about me in the same way I was thinking about her. That thought warmed a fire in me before I brought the mug back to my lips, being careful to avoid the whipped cream mustache which had ended up on my lips just seconds before.

Although the warm liquid brought some warmth back to my body after having been out on the ice and in the cold weather, I knew the heat that was coursing through my veins was because of the look she had given me. I couldn't remember the last time I just had fun with someone of the opposite sex, versus it being some quick one-night stand after meeting at a bar, because I had deemed myself too busy to form an actual relationship.

And that thought gave me pause. Did I want something deeper than just a one-night stand? I didn't know, but I knew I wanted to see more of Nicole, who made it clear she wasn't ready for anything remotely close to a relationship. That was understandable, given the circumstances she found herself in.

"Nicole." She had been gazing out of one of the windows in the bar and turned her attention to me. "I've been thinking. I enjoy spending time with you."

A curious look appeared on her face before the corners of her lips formed into a smile. "I enjoy spending with you too."

I took a deep breath as I braced myself for her to say no. "I was wondering if you were interested in having a fling." I could see her processing my words in her mind, but she hadn't said no, so I kept talking. "We could continue having fun together while we're both at the Holiday Springs Resort, and it would be no strings attached. I mean, we're already doing the first part of that now."

I debated how to approach this. Wanting to tell her I was hoping for more, but also not wanting to scare her away, if that's not what she was interested in, because at this point, I would take whatever she wanted to give. I tapped my fingertips on a table, trying to find the right words to say, instead of just spitting them out. Funny how being around her turned me into a bumbling fool. "Would you say we have chemistry?"

She nodded her head. "I felt it when you spoke to me at the front desk when we were checking in."

"I felt it too. What I'm trying to say is: I was wondering if you want to do something more than just hang out. We can see how our chemistry works in the bedroom too." I almost rolled my eyes at myself because it came out way cheesier than I was expecting, but at least it was out there. Normally, the one-night stands I had experienced progressed naturally, depending on when and where we were. This, on the other hand, I wanted to approach carefully. This would be a fling which would be occurring over several days versus one night in the sack. So, I wanted to make sure we understood one another.

"Barrett, are you alluding to what I think you're alluding to?"

"What do you think I'm alluding to?" I wanted to hear her say the words out loud.

She leant closer to me. "You want to have sex with me?" Her voice came out huskier than normal, and her words just above a whisper, trying her best not to draw attention to us.

"Sort of? More like a fling, since we'd be hanging out

around the resort as well. You don't want anything serious, and I don't want anything serious. Doesn't mean we shouldn't have some fun while we are here. That is, only if you're okay with it."

Based on the way her eyes were moving, I assumed Nicole was tossing the idea back and forth in her mind like a tennis match. She looked down at her feet, and I had a feeling she was going to say no.

"I like this idea."

I did a double take. She liked the idea of having a fling?

"Are you sure?" I asked, waiting with bated breath for her to confirm.

"Yeah, I mean, it's not something I normally do. But when in Rome, right? I've lived my life carefully planned for so long, and there is nothing wrong with a little spontaneity and living life on the edge a bit, if that makes sense."

I just stared at her. I didn't expect this conversation to go as well as it was.

"This sounds like a deal. Do we shake hands to seal it?"

I shook my head. "I was thinking more along the lines of a kiss, like the one we shared last night."

"I'm not opposed to that." Her voice was still lower than normal, and the tone was sending the blood away from my brain.

I stood up and sat next to her. I surveyed the room quickly, making sure our server had no intention of coming back to interrupt us. I placed my hand on her cheek and leaned in to touch her lips to mine. When our lips met, my tongue made its way into her mouth, and I could taste the hot chocolate she had just consumed, but it was also mixed with a taste I was quickly beginning to realize was all her own. I felt her hands move up my chest, and her fingers grasped my cashmere sweater as if she were trying to draw us even closer together. I just knew she had to be feeling how hard my heart was pounding because of her touch.

The kiss ended naturally on its own, and we broke apart. I looked down at her and still found her eyes closed, as if she were trying to prolong the feeling of the kiss we had just shared. I watched her eyes float back open.

"Well, that was lovely," she said, and touched her fingers to her lips.

"I don't know if lovely can adequately describe what I'm feeling right now." I raked a hand through my hair and took a deep breath, trying to calm my erratically beating heart. "How could that be better than the kiss from last night?"

"I-I don't know." I found her staring down at the hot chocolate. Perhaps she was wondering the same thing I was. How did every time we touch just keep getting better and better?

## SEVEN

# NICOLE

I was supposed to be writing a bestselling romance book, but I was still stuck in the same place I had been before. You'd think because I already had a basis for my story that I could just pick up where it left off and turn it into something great, but I was still struggling. I couldn't think of anything. I had tried plotting, and that didn't work. Free writing was the next thing I tried, but not even that was working. I ran my hands across my face, trying to relieve some tension building in my head. I needed to have this story drafted fast.

I could have blamed it on circumstances, and I could have blamed it on the fact I still was somewhat in a funk after my breakup with Chris. But in the back of my head, I knew people had already pre-ordered this book. In fact, it was looking like it might be the most pre-orders I'd had on a book to date. Thankfully, I had taken a few months off for my wedding that didn't materialize, so I didn't have to push my release date back—at least not yet. I didn't want to risk losing the orders I already gathered for this book. Yet I still had nothing.

Figuring I needed to find something else to do, I called my sister. It didn't take her long to pick up the phone.

"How's your vacation going? Or did you want to talk about book stuff?" I could hear Angie doing something in the background while she was talking to me.

"Nah, talking about vacation stuff is fine. And I can't complain about it." I paused for a beat. "Partially because I met up with check-in guy again."

"You did what?" That was enough to stop her from doing whatever she was doing. It was clear based on the tone of her voice she was in shock from my statement.

"Yeah, I guess I spoke it into existence, but I saw him again when I wandered out to get a drink from the bar the night I arrived. And we ended up grabbing drinks at the bar and talking most of the evening." I twirled the end of my ponytail around my index finger.

I noticed her quick intake of breath before she blurted out, "It has been months since you've mentioned another man! So please tell me you found out more about him."

"You know the reason I haven't mentioned anyone is because I had no intention of meeting someone anytime soon. I was doing just fine on my own. And was busy between the cancelled wedding stuff, moving out of Chris's apartment, moving in with you, and then finding an apartment for myself once again." The whole thing had been a blessing in disguise, because I had found an even better apartment than the one I'd had before I took the leap with Chris.

"That's true. Are you even ready to date anyone? Especially since this guy kind of fell into your lap based on the bit you told me? I wouldn't blame you if you weren't, given everything that happened with Chris. And even that was way more amicable than I expected."

That's because there was nothing to fight for, I told myself, but decided not to share it with Angie. It was almost too easy to get my things and move out of the apartment Chris and I had briefly shared. We both ended up paying the amount we owed for the wedding and paid our parents back for their monetary gifts to us. We returned the gifts our guests had bought and told everyone who could not make it to the wedding there wasn't a wedding, but we were happy with the turn of events. Although I had declared I wanted nothing to do with anyone else, when I talked to Barrett, my feelings changed. Still, putting myself out there made me nervous.

"I know. I'm happy I came to an agreement with Chris so I could take this trip and not him."

"Honestly, you deserve it, and he broke your heart so he can kick rocks. Tell me more about this mystery guy!"

I adjusted my body, folding my legs underneath myself. "His name is Barrett, and he lives in New York City. He works as an investment banker."

"New York City isn't far away from Philadelphia. I'm just saying."

"I know it's not. But we are nowhere near that point. In fact, we talked about having a fling while we were here."

"Oh, really? I'm shocked you went along with it since you're a serial monogamous-relationship type of person."

I stopped for a second to figure out what she was getting at. She wasn't wrong. "I know, but I want to try something a little different. What I've been doing before isn't exactly working."

"You're right, it's not working. A fling certainly seems different. If your definition of a fling means you should both be banging each other's brains into the next century, then yes."

My snort turned into a fit full of giggles. It took a moment for them to subside. "You're hilarious."

"After all, the best way to get over someone is to get under someone else."

I chuckled but kept the fact I had thought the same thing a couple of days ago to myself. Plus, I wanted nothing to do with

Chris. "But what if there isn't much to get over? I spent most of the last few months trying to figure out where Chris and I went wrong. Honestly, I feel like I was more hurt at the fact our relationship ended because of all the time we spent together versus being hurt I was no longer with him. If that makes sense."

"And that is even more reason to get under Barrett."

I pinched the bridge of my nose and sighed. "Well, I already agreed to the fling, so I assume it's just a matter of time at this point."

I could hear her whooping and hollering in the background. "Nic, you're a grown woman. You can do what you want, and I didn't want to come across as if I was pressuring you. But I'm so happy you agreed to get down and dirty with him. Enjoy yourself, and if he's the person you want to spend some time with, so be it. Just be careful about getting hurt."

I noted the change in the tone of her voice. It went from friendly best friend to big sister 'I'm about to lay some advice on you, so you better listen up.' Even though we were both grown and she was only older than me by two years, this happened every so often. When I was younger, I used to get annoyed about it, but now I usually listened to what she said and weighed my options.

"I think I know what you're getting at, but feel free to spell it out for me."

"Like I mentioned earlier, you are a serial monogamous-relationship type of person who doesn't get together with someone on a whim. This is a whole different experience for you, but I don't want you to get attached to him since you guys already agreed to break it off once your stays come to an end. And this is coming on the heels of a broken engagement less than a year old. All I'm saying is to be careful."

I let her words hang in the air for a few moments before I replied. "I will."

I quickly hung up the phone with my sister and knew I needed to get out of my room for a bit. I walked over to the phone in my cabin and pressed the appropriate number for guest services.

"Hello, you've reached guest services at the Holiday Springs Resort. Melina speaking."

"Hi, Melina, I was wondering if you had any recommendations for somewhat quiet places where someone could work on their computer."

"Hm. If I had to recommend a place, I would recommend Java Junction in town. It's a cafe that's not too far away from the resort. But if that wouldn't work, you could always work near the fireplace in the lodge. It might be a bit busy with everyone checking in and out, but you'd probably get the same level of noise at Java Junction. Oh, and if you go, I would recommend you try their pumpkin spice latte."

I smiled at her suggestion and rolled the idea around in my head. "This is super helpful. Thank you."

"No problem. Is there anything else I could help you with?"

"Nope, that would be all."

"Awesome. I hope you have a great day!"

I hung up the phone and began packing the things I needed to take with me to Java Junction.

## EIGHT

## BARRETT

Although I tried, I couldn't stop thinking about her. I knew part of that was due to my ability to overanalyze situations. Helpful when it came to work, less helpful when it came to get someone or something off of your mind. I couldn't remember the last time I had thought about something other than work first thing in the morning. I stretched my arms above my head, trying to force my body to wake up. I leant over to check the time on the bedside table.

I squinted and saw it was 9:30 am, confirming I had slept in for the first time in a very long time. It took a few minutes of convincing myself, but I hopped out of bed and threw on my gym clothes. Although I didn't really want to exercise right now, I wanted to keep up my routine. I knew if I didn't, I would slack off when I got back home, making it harder to fall back into the routine I started since I'd began focusing more on keeping fit several years ago.

About twenty minutes later, I was lifting weights in front of one of the gym mirrors. When I took a short breather after another set of reps, my phone buzzed in my pocket. I pulled it out and noticed it was an email for work. I debated with myself whether it made sense to read it. Curiosity won out. I read the email, sent a quick response—thankful it wasn't anything more pressing which would require me to hop in front of my computer in order to answer—put my phone back in my pocket, and went back to working out. Once I finished my last round of bicep curls, I wiped off the weights and headed out of the gym. A hot shower was waiting for me back in my hotel room.

Once that was complete and I had changed my clothes, I headed back to the bedroom slash living area and sat down at my desk in the room. I debated whether it was a good idea to contact Nicole to see what she was doing. But I also didn't want to seem pushy, as if she had to spend every waking moment with me while she was here. But my mom removed any debate I was having with myself because I answered the phone when she called.

"MOM, EVERYTHING IS FINE." I was starting to think she was checking up on me because the likelihood of me going on vacation was nil and that I must have fallen and hit my head.

"I know, but I'm your mom, and I'll always worry about you. Plus, did you hear about the snowfall the Poconos is supposed to get in a few days?"

I had paid little attention to the weather since I'd arrived, but this didn't surprise me much, given where I was. "Now, we are in the mountains, so I assume a crazy snowfall total isn't out of the question, especially at this time of year."

When I'd booked this trip, I was worried about going to Holiday Springs Resort, let alone smack dab in between Christmas and New Year's. If I hadn't gone, I wouldn't have met

Nicole, which was proving to be the biggest highlight of this vacation.

"Barrett? Are you there?"

"Yeah. Sorry, I'm still here. Can you repeat what you said?"

"I asked you how the trip was going? Meet any interesting people? Done any cool things?"

I licked my lips, thinking about whether I should tell my mother about Nicole. I mean, what was the harm? It's not like they would get a chance to meet each other, anyway. "Yes, I have done quite a few things, and there is one person in particular I've met who stands out above everyone else."

"Does this person happened to be a woman?"

"How did you figure that out?"

"You can call it mother's intuition. You could also say I just know you really, really well and could hear how you lit up when you mentioned her. Whatever you want to use."

I rolled my eyes but smiled. "Mom, it's nothing serious. It's not like Nicole is coming to Thanksgiving dinner next year. We've just met and are having fun here. Nothing more, nothing less." I was pretty sure those words came out faster than Usain Bolt, which made me sound ridiculous.

"If that's what helps you get through the day, dear. Nicole, huh? That's a pretty name. There's something about her that has caught your attention. I can't even remember the last time you sounded this excited about someone."

She wasn't wrong about that either. I rarely brought up anyone I was casually dating, let alone someone I hadn't slept with. For some reason, this felt right. It felt right telling my mother about Nicole.

Just as I was about to think of a response, my phone buzzed my hand. I looked down and saw it was Gary calling me. It wasn't unheard of for him to call me during off hours, but I found it strange he was calling me when I was supposed to be on vacation. A vacation he wanted me to go on.

"Hey, Mom. I gotta go. My boss is on the other line."

"Okay. I'll talk to you soon."

With that, I clicked off and with a few clicks, I had Gary set up on speaker in my hotel room.

"Gary, is everything okay?"

"Yes." His voice was gruff and somewhat impatient, not a tone our office was unfamiliar with. "I know you're on vacation, but a couple of questions came up from some clients you're working with, and I was wondering if you would hop on and get them sorted."

Normally this wouldn't have annoyed me, and I would have been happy to oblige him. But I had still been debating if I should reach out to Nicole after I got off the phone with my mom, and this was holding me up. "Yeah, sure. I should be able to get on within the next twenty minutes or so."

"Great." He paused for a moment, and I wondered if I should be the one to initiate us to hang up. "How's the vacation going? Gina asked about it after I mentioned you were going. She's been bugging me about going even more now that I told her you booked the trip on her suggestion."

Keep it short and sweet, Pierce. "It's a wonderful place with plenty to do. I'm sure your wife would love to come here."

"Noted." He coughed to clear his throat. "That will be all. And, ah, sorry to disturb you while you're supposed to be out of the office."

Gary was apologizing for disturbing me? That was new. "Don't worry about it. Have a good rest of your day." And with that, we hung up.

I had just placed my phone down on my desk when it buzzed again.

"I don't know if I've ever had this many people contact me

in this short length of time," I mumbled to myself. It was a text from Nicole.

**Nicole**: *Hey, I hoped that a change of scenery would help me write this book. Want to join me at Java Junction in about fifteen minutes?*

I smiled. Looks like the debate I was having with myself was pointless because her text message was my answer.

## NINE

## NICOLE

I still hadn't made a move to type anything up, but I felt better being in a new location versus being surrounded by the walls in my cabin. I had set up shop at the Java Junction, the little rustic cafe in town Melina had recommended to me. Although she had recommended their pumpkin spice latte, I figured I would try the chai latte, and it did not disappoint. I debated grabbing something small to eat to give me the inspiration to write, or it could just be something to take my mind off of the fact I wasn't writing anything.

And here I was again, staring at nothing on my computer screen, willing a sign to appear to point me toward what I should type.

"Nicole?"

I looked up and found Barrett smiling at me. "Hey! Glad you could make it," I said, displaying more enthusiasm than I felt due to my current situation.

"Me too. I was glad you mentioned coming down here, but I just had a couple of work things thrown into my lap. So, you had excellent timing. Are you sure I won't disturb you?"

"Of course not. Writing sometimes is so isolating, so it's nice to have some company. Wait. Aren't you supposed to not be working while on vacation?"

Barrett gave me a small grin before he said, "Shouldn't I say the same thing about you?"

I nodded my head in a yeah-you-have-a-good-point type of way. But he didn't have to point it out. "*Touché.* Well, why don't you get comfortable, and we can get started?"

Barrett thought about it for a moment and sent a smile my way. "Happy to." He set his bag down next to me before he turned back to me. "Is there anything I can get you? A refill? Food?"

"A refill would be lovely. I had a chai tea latte, and one of their famous homemade cinnamon rolls would be amazing."

"A chai tea latte and cinnamon roll coming right up."

"Thanks." His parting smile sent quivers through my body as Angie's words about sleeping with him spun around in my head. I glanced over at him, and he was the next person in line to have his order taken. We had agreed to the fling yesterday, but he hadn't taken the opportunity to do anything more than kiss me. Was he having regrets?

My thoughts fought amongst themselves in my mind and distracted me to the point where I didn't even realize Barrett had come back with two mugs in his hand until he was placing them on the table. "I have to run back and get everything else."

"Do you need any help?"

"Nope, I got it."

I nodded just before he walked away, and I imagined what sex might be like with him. Would he be a gentle lover, or would he do things hard and fast? I chuckled under my breath and silently scolded myself. I needed to get my head on straight.

"What's up?"

"Nothing." I took a sip of the warm chai latte he had placed in front of me. As I was placing the cup back down on the table, he slid into the booth to sit next to me, and images based on the last time he had done this sprang to mind.

"Are you sure?" He placed more emphasis on the question by placing his hand just above my knee. I almost begged him to go higher, although the mountain of clothes we both had on would restrict us both. His hand definitely had a mind of its own, because when I didn't respond right away, his hand moved about an inch higher and an inch closer to my inner thigh. Then he started making small circles as his fingers crept toward the spot where I had hoped he would eventually make his acquaintance known. My eyes moved from the motions his hands were making on me to look up at him. The small smirk that played on his lips told me he knew exactly what he was doing to me and was enjoying it.

And that was when he had provided me the answer to the question about whether or not he still wanted me in the same way I wanted him.

"Yep. Everything is... perfect."

"I'm glad." His hand moved across my inner thigh a few more times and got dangerously close to my center. Although I was wearing jeans, I could feel the anticipation building within me as I wondered what he was going to do next. I felt a sense of emptiness when he removed his hand to help set up his work area. That was when I let out a restrained sigh.

"Is that what it sounds like?" I barely heard it because of how low he had spoken and the noise in the coffee shop.

I looked over at him and leant closer to him, almost whispering in his ear. "Is that what *what* sounds like?"

"When you're getting turned on. Duly noted. There's more where that came from."

Although he hadn't said much, I could hear the promises laced throughout his words. He knew exactly what he had been doing by building up the foreplay between us, and when we would finally come together as one, both literally and figuratively, it would be explosive.

---

"ARE you sure you want to do this?" I asked, preparing myself for Barrett to say this was the last thing he wanted to do.

We had finished up what we wanted to do at Java Junction, and I was so happy I had started piecing a story together through all the jumble of documents I had on my computer. I brought up the idea of us doing a version of a paint and sip class at the resort, but instead of us having to paint the same thing with a class, we got to choose our own projects with instruction from the teachers in the room. Barrett seemed to be game for it, but I didn't know if he was just being nice and really wanted to leave and never look back.

"Yes. I don't get much of an opportunity to explore my creative side, so I figured why not do it on vacation? This is a great idea." He paused. "And if I really suck, there's enough alcohol for me to hide my shame."

I couldn't stop myself from bursting out laughing. It had just clicked in my mind that that's how I spent my time with him: either laughing at something he said or just enjoying his company. The thought made me giddy inside. I helped him secure his apron, and he helped me secure mine. We took our time picking out which arts and crafts project we wanted to work on and were fortunate enough to not have to share a table with anyone else due to how many people had decided to take the class. Once we were settled at our table, we waited for our teachers to give the first instruction before we got started.

"You know, this is oddly relaxing." Barrett said after a few moments. We had been concentrating on our projects, instead of trying to make conversation, yet the silence didn't feel awkward at all. It felt as if we had known each other way longer than we had.

"Did you think it was going to be stressful?"

"Yes. After all, I'm trying to impress you, and I don't know how I'm doing right now."

His words caused a rush of heat to flood my body. I hoped a blush wasn't appearing on my cheeks, but because I could feel my face warming up, that wasn't a bet I was willing to take.

"Which project did you pick?"

Barrett held up a wooden square-shaped container. "Figured I might be able to use this at work. Can never have too many places to hold pencils and pens. Thought I could make it festive to celebrate the holidays. You?"

"Just a circular bar tray that says celebrate. Figured I'd keep it somewhat simple, and I could use the tray all year round."

Barrett dipped his head, and his eyes moved from the soon-to-be decorated tray to me. I could feel the electricity in his gaze. I smiled as I tried to ignore it, because I knew anyone in our general vicinity would probably feel the magnetism between us too. Our attention was drawn away from one another and forced to focus on our teachers, because it was time to listen to our instructor explain the next steps. We both wanted to stain the wood before adding our respective decorations to our crafts.

While we waited for the stain to dry. One of the teachers came by and asked us what type of wine or beer we wanted to drink. After I chose a glass of white wine and Barrett chose a beer, we sat back on our stools and checked out everyone in the room around us before I turned the attention back to what I wanted to know.

"The stunt you pulled earlier was mean."

Although we hadn't known each other for a long time, the look on his face almost made me roll my eyes. It was a look of fake innocence. "I have no idea what you're talking about."

I glanced around the room before I placed my hand on his knee. "Oh, but I think you do."

Instead of taking my time like he had done at Java Junction, I made a beeline to feeling him up in his jeans. I heard him mumble a few choice words, and I smiled as I felt him grow harder beneath my touch. His words were music to my ears that headed straight down to my nipples as I felt them harden against the restraint that my bra caused.

"It's not so much fun when the tables are turned, is it?"

"Sometime soon, you're going to pay for that."

And I couldn't wait.

TEN

BARRETT

"This might be tacky for me to say, especially on a date. But does this menu seem overpriced to you?" Nicole asked just above a whisper. We had just put our orders in at the Drunken Yeti after dropping off our work gear and arts and craft projects in our rooms. I had then picked Nicole up from her cabin and headed into town, after telling her I wanted to check out this bar just because of its name. It was the definition of a hole in a wall, but I didn't think either of us minded, outside of the high price for drinks.

When I asked Nicole to come with me to the Drunken Yeti, calling it a date wasn't the first thing that came to mind. I couldn't remember the last time I had been on a date, let alone one as enjoyable as the time I've spent with her.

"Nope, I think you hit that right on the head. Even though, let's be real, these prices aren't much different from the price of drinks we could get in New York City."

Nicole shrugged. "I would say New York is a bit more expensive, but you're the native." She took a second to look around the bar. "There's one thing I will say about this place. It definitely has character."

I held up the glass of water the server had brought right after we sat down. "Cheers to that."

A giggle escaped her lips as she clinked her glass with mine. "That being said, I'm happy we came here. When I go on vacation or visit a place, I love to explore the local culture of the area. You can just stay on resort property, or you can go where some locals hang out and get a feel for what life is like here."

"Well, that's a great perspective to have. I don't travel much for work, and everyone knows I don't usually do vacations."

"And why is that?"

It was a good question. What was wrong with taking a vacation? "I think I tie a lot of my self-worth to working. How many clients I had, bonuses I was awarded, praise I received. A lot of my focus was put into advancing in my field, so I never really thought about taking a break. Well, unless I was sick and had to. Even then, I still found myself answering emails."

"And you've been going at this neck-breaking pace for years?"

I nodded.

"I'm shocked your performance only just started suffering."

I didn't respond right away because our server just handed us the beers we ordered. Once she walked away, I turned back to Nicole. "You sound like you have some experience with this?"

"I do. At one point, I was publishing books every three weeks or so."

"Now I don't know much about the publishing industry, but that sounds like it would be a crazy schedule to keep up."

Nicole smirked at me. "You're one to talk. But, yes, it was pretty insane. I was writing, editing, publishing, doing promotion for them every three to four weeks. Rinse and repeat for at least a year." She paused. "Maybe it was for a year and a half."

"What happened?"

"Writer's block. Similar to what I was experiencing when I arrived here but worse. At least while I'm here, I'm actually attempting to write. I didn't open up my laptop for months after that incident. I was fortunate enough that, because I had pushed out so many books in a short period of time. They were making me money, and there wasn't a dire need for me to continue going at the pace I was going. Some writers thrive in that environment, and that's great. I didn't, and that's okay too. Although I will admit I gained quite a few fans due to my writing that fast."

"So essentially it was a blessing and a curse."

"Yeah, I would say so."

I put my beer to my lips but didn't take my eyes off of her. I placed the beer back down on the table. "At first, I was kind of annoyed my boss wanted me to take a vacation."

"That might be the first time I've ever heard someone utter those words." Her eyes cut over to me as the corners of her lips lifted. The smirk didn't last long because she too took another sip of her beer.

"I'm full of surprises."

"You aren't wrong about that." Her eyes told me there was more to the statement than she was letting on. Thinking it might potentially do more harm than good if I asked her more, I refrained.

But there was something I wanted her to know. "I still want to take you out to a nice dinner."

"I wouldn't say no to that. We could go to the Mountain Lake Bar & Restaurant."

"That sounds good. I did want to try it at some point." I mentally made a note.

"I know that is also a great place to watch the firework display over the lake, because of the huge windows in the restaurant."

That's right. New Year's Eve was just around the corner. "I'll keep that in mind. Do you have plans for tomorrow?"

Nicole didn't answer right away. While I waited for her response, I pleaded to myself she would be free to make it. We had been hanging out regularly, but even that didn't seem to be enough.

"I need to take some time in the morning and do some work-related things, but I'll be free after that. What did you have in mind?"

"It's a surprise."

"Oh, come on. You can tell me what it is."

"Do you really want to know? And ruin the surprise?"

"I do like surprises...."

"Then I won't tell you. But I have a feeling you're going to enjoy yourself."

I watched as our server came back to our table and quickly asked if we were doing well. When we confirmed we were, he walked away. As I was taking a sip of the beer, Nicole mentioned, "You know, I don't think I said anything while we were finishing up our crafts, but you did a phenomenal job with yours."

"Thanks. I thought it was decent, and it was hard to mess up based on the instructions they gave us. Your tray came out beautifully." Just like you, I added to myself.

"It was pretty. Can't wait to use it whenever I have my next get-together. Oh, I need to go to the bathroom. I'll be right back." She stood up and hurried away from the table.

Even though she didn't say it, my mind drifted back to the harsh reality that this had an end date. I wouldn't be around for the next get-together she held at her apartment in Philly, and that stung unexpectedly.

A new thought fluttered in my mind. It wondered what life would be like if we might be able to make this work if we wanted to. We both enjoyed spending time with one another and had gotten to know each other over the series of dates we had been on. Could this work outside of the little bubble we created here at the Holiday Springs Resort? Philadelphia wasn't that far from New York City, and public transportation made it easy to get to one another. A bunch of scenarios floated around in my head, but one notion brought them all to a halt.

This also hedged on whether Nicole was willing to take a risk by dating again. I glanced up at the ceiling. As someone who analyzed everything by nature, and for my job, there were still too many variables which need to be answered before I could reach a conclusion.

## ELEVEN

## NICOLE

The next morning, I found myself staring out of the window across the room from my desk. Snow was lightly falling outside, providing a sense of tranquility. I'd spent most of the morning writing, but now my brain was pretty shot in terms of what to do next. I stretched my arms above my head and was interrupted by my cellphone's ping.

**Barrett:** *I have a surprise for you. All you have to do is call the front desk and ask for the honeymoon special to be delivered to your cabin around 4:30pm, and I'll handle the rest.*

He had piqued my interest. What in the world could he be planning? Part of me wanted to look up what the honeymoon special was, but I didn't want to ruin whatever Barrett had up his sleeve. Plus, what good was it to have a honeymoon cabin and not enjoy all of the amenities and perks that came with it?

A couple of hours later, I had another text message from Barrett.

**Barrett:** *I'm sure you've been working hard, but this is also supposed to be a vacation... for both of us. Meet me at the Lake-view Wellness Spa at 2:45pm.*

His words made me even more excited about the plans he

had made. I threw on some clothes and my winter gear and drove to the spa.

When I arrived, I was shocked to not find him there. He had thrown out the idea of a massage during one of our previous text messages, but I didn't know he was being serious about it. I grabbed my phone out of my coat pocket to see if I had a message from him, but saw nothing.

"Ms.? How might I help you?" The receptionist at the front desk greeted me with a polite smile.

"I think I have an appointment at 3? I assume it's under Nicole Ford."

"Ah, yes. I think your boyfriend booked it for you last night." Visions of what occurred when I checked in ran through my mind and how quick I was to correct the woman at the front desk about my relationship status. This seemed different. I didn't mind her assuming Barrett was my boyfriend.

"Please just fill out these forms, and we'll call you when it's time to head to the back."

I filled out the forms, and since my name still hadn't been called, I checked my messages again. And to my surprise, I had one from Barrett.

**Barrett:** *How is everything going?*

**Me:** *Good so far. I thought you were coming to do a massage too.*

**Barrett:** *Nope, I had some things to wrap up, but I'll see you after. Hope it's as relaxing as it sounds.*

"Ms. Ford?"

I had been so distracted by my phone I hadn't heard the woman who was now standing at the front desk call out. "Um. Yes? That's me." My words came out as more of a question than a statement.

"My name is Isabelle, and I'll be your masseuse for today.

I'll take those papers from you and get them sorted for you. Please follow me."

I stood up and followed Isabelle once she walked around the front desk and headed toward a door across the room from us. She quickly turned the doorknob and held it open for me while I walked through. I followed her down a longer hallway lined with peaceful and serene photos. The light soft music playing in the background reminded of some music I'd listened to when I tried meditation. I made a note to myself that that was something I needed to get back into when I got home as a way to help manage stress.

"Have you had a massage done before?"

"Oh, yes, plenty of times."

That gave Isabelle a reason to chuckle. "Since you're a pro, I probably don't have to go through all the steps." She paused and turned to a door on the right. "Ms. Ford, just through this door, is our locker room. In there are freshly cleaned robes and slippers. You know the drill. And two doors down the hallway on your right will be our room for your session. Is there anything else that you might need?"

I shook my head and watched as Isabelle left me alone with my thoughts. She was right that I knew the drill. I took off all of my clothes besides my panties and placed my belongings in one of the lockers.

I walked into the room Isabelle had pointed out to me would be the room she would give me the massage in. She gave me a moment to get settled on the massage table before she came back in and got to work.

I felt like Jell-O after the massage Isabelle had given me. I couldn't remember the last time I had felt this relaxed. All my worries, all my troubles had faded away as she took her time working out every knot in my shoulders and back. Once I dressed and had everything I came in with, I walked out to the front desk.

The receptionist greeted me again with a smile, and when I told her to charge it to my room, she shook her head. "This is already taken care of. I hope you have a lovely rest of your day." My head jerked back involuntarily. Barrett had paid for the massage for me. Part of me was happy that he did. The other part of me felt a little weird about it, but that was something I could dissect later.

I thanked the receptionist and turned to exit the spa. As I was about to leave the building altogether, I heard someone shout, "Ms. Ford!"

I turned around, and the receptionist was jogging after me with an envelope in her hand. "I'm so sorry I forgot to give this to you. Have a good evening." And with that, she left me standing in the spa's entranceway with the envelope in my hand.

A small smile appeared on my lips as I tore open the flap and pulled the note card out of the envelope.

*Meet me at your cabin for an evening full of surprises.*
*Barrett.*

I dashed to my car, envelope in tow, and slowly drove back to my cabin, because I was attempting to avoid the snow which was starting to pick up. When I reached my cabin, I took my key and opened the door. I was greeted by rose petals in the doorway. I followed the trail to the bedroom and living area. I cursed quietly to myself because the ping on my phone had made me jump.

**Barrett**: *I'm running a little behind. I should be there in about 10 minutes. Why don't you go find the surprise the staff left for you in the bathroom?*

I bit my lip as I put my phone back in my pocket and walked into my bathroom. There were all the fixings for a warm bubble bath. A couple of bath bombs, some champagne, and more rose petals surround the tub.

Who was I to let all these things go to waste? I drew the bath and organized things to my liking. Just as I was about to turn off the faucet, there was a knock on my cabin door. Knowing who it was, I couldn't stop the smile from appearing on my face. I made my way to the hallway and opened the door for the man who had started all of this.

Barrett appeared on the other side of the door with his arms full of stuff. His windswept brown hair had flakes of snow in it. "Looks like you've been shopping," I said, as I stepped back to let him into the cabin.

"If you only knew," he said as he made his way into the small living area. "Most of this stuff is food."

"I thought we were having room service delivered to us this evening? That's what I vaguely remember being a part of the honeymoon package."

"It is. I just bought some extra snacks and things in case we are snowed in for a day or so."

I did a double take. "Wait a minute. Snowed in?"

He glanced back at me after setting the bags on the counter. He then took off his backpack, which I assumed was filled with some of his personal possessions. "Yeah, we're supposed to be getting a snowstorm late this evening and into tomorrow. I figured the resort will have things back up and running pretty quickly, because they're used to this type of thing. But just in case, we didn't want to wander out for food, we were set. Some things I knew you'd like based on what you ordered when we've been together, but some things I guessed."

"Are you always this prepared?" I asked, slightly changing the subject. I folded my arms and leaned on the counter. I didn't try to hide the fact that he had impressed me. "I usually try to have Plan A, Plan B, and Plan C when it comes to life. Even though at this very moment, I'm going with the flow."

"I would say that I am." He continued to remove the food from their bags.

"I usually do the same thing. Yet, here I am loving how this going with the flow is working," I said, gesturing to him and back to myself. "I should probably hop in the tub before the water cools down."

"Great. I'll just wrap up putting these things away, and I'll see you in a minute."

I assumed he was alluded to joining me in the bathroom when he was done, but I didn't ask any more questions. I left him to finish his tasks and walked into the second part of what I hoped would be a relaxing evening that ended in some fun. After I got naked, I lowered the lights in the bathroom and stepped into the tub. The warm water was the icing on the cake of my already relaxed body. Any stress that remained after the massage oozed out of my pores as I caused small ripples in the water. I didn't know how long I was in there before Barrett softly knocked on the door and entered when I told him to come in.

## TWELVE

## BARRETT

Although the lights were low, I could still see the outline of her body lying in the tub, and that was all I needed to make the blood rush from my head to somewhere further south.

The dimmed lights almost caused a candle-like effect in the room, further setting the mood I was hoping to create. I walked further into the bathroom.

"Hey," I whispered. She looked over at me and smiled before beckoning me over with her hand. That was when she noticed the glass in my hand.

"You brought me a glass of champagne? But I thought there was one in here—" Her voice trailed off as her eyes looked over and found the bottle the hotel staff had mentioned they were leaving earlier.

"This is white wine. I figured we could open the bottle of champagne later, if you wanted to." I handed her the glass before walking back over to the doorjamb to lean on it.

"Oh! Chardonnay. My favorite." She put the glass up to her lips once more, and I noticed the low lighting did nothing to stop the sparkle in her eye. And that was before she looked over at me and grinned. "Thank you so much for today. I don't know if I've ever had someone go all out for me like this. Ever."

"You're welcome. It's my pleasure. And the evening is just getting started." I gave her another smile and turned to leave the bathroom.

"Barrett." My name on her lips was smooth like the white wine that she had her glass. "Would you like to join me?"

I was hoping she would ask that. I grabbed my phone out of my pocket and saw that dinner wouldn't arrive for another hour, so I had plenty of time. I whipped off my sweater and unbuckled my jeans. I looked up and found her watching my every move.

"You know it's rude to stare, right?"

"I. Don't. Care."

I chuckled but said nothing. I had planned on doing the same thing to her. After all, fair was fair.

"As long as you're okay with me studying your stunning body once we get out of the tub, then I don't mind."

"Deal."

She leaned forward to give me some room in the tub, and once we both settled, she leaned her head back on me and let out a deep breath. The first scent that drifted to my nose was something familiar yet strange. If I had to place it, I would say it was a mixture of vanilla and lavender and something else, something I couldn't quite put my finger on. What I did know was it was a soothing scent that helped me feel even more relaxed.

"Do you use something that is lavender and vanilla scented?"

She glanced up at me from out of the corner of her eye before looking back at water. "Yep, those are some of the scents that are in one of the lotions I use and my conditioner. You have a great sense of smell."

"Thanks, I think." I licked my lips when she looked back at

me. She laid her body on mine, and I said, "I can't remember the last time I took a bath. Usually it's too hard for to me fit in one because of my height."

"It must be so hard being over six feet tall."

"You have no idea. I'd also say this is the best bath I've ever had because of present company."

She laughed. "Is that right?"

"Mmhmm." My attention to the conversation waned as she slowly adjusted herself, rubbing herself against my crotch. Once she stopped her ministrations, she let out a small giggle which told me she had done it on purpose. "You thought that was funny? Don't forget, I still haven't paid you back for the little stunt you pulled during our paint and sip class."

"That was just revenge for what you did to me at Java Junction."

"But that wasn't meant to be a tease. That was me giving you a little taste of what was to come."

"I'm still waiting for what is coming... especially when I thought it was going to be me by now."

I could see the outline of the top of her breasts poking out of the water as her breathing got shallower. I was glad this was having the same effect on her as it was having on me.

My hand moved up and down her arm, which was leaning on the edge of the tub. I softly dipped my hand into the water and searched until I found what I was looking for. My hand started massaging her breast, and when I heard the same sigh she'd made in Java Junction, it drove even more blood to my cock. My other hand found its way to her other breast, and I felt both of her nipples become as hard as pebbles in my hand. When my lips landed on her neck and sucked, it was as if the floodgates had opened up. She couldn't stop withering against my body, nor could she stop the noises that were escaping her lips.

"Please," she said in between heavy sighs. The noises she was making almost made me groan.

I stopped the kissing and sucking along the side of her neck she had given me access to. "Please what?" I wanted to hear her say the words.

"Please don't stop."

"I had no intention of stopping. In fact, I wanted to kick it up a notch." I buried my face into her neck as one of my hands traveled lower, to where I had given her a small sample of what was to come earlier today.

I lightly touched the skin just above her mound before going further down, to the place where I thought she wanted me most. I soon learned how right I was.

The moans that came from her were like music to my ears. As I strummed my fingers across her heat, she threw her head back, which I then took as a sign to find that spot on her neck that had forced her to spin out of control.

"Uh... Barrett!" she screamed, and I knew she was getting close. Another moan left her lips just before her body slowly relaxed in my embrace. I left small kisses along her neck and collarbone as she tried to bring herself back down to Earth. She murmured some noises to herself I wasn't even sure she realized she had. "Wow."

"Did that make up for earlier today?" I asked. I couldn't help but smile because I had helped place her in this state of relaxation.

"More than made up for it." She was still mumbling her words, but I could understand that clearly. It took a few more moments before she realized her surroundings. "Wait, Barrett, you didn't—"

"This wasn't for me. It was for you, and that was only the first round. Let's get both of us out of the tub and into some dry clothes. We're going to need some food to sustain us tonight."

## THIRTEEN

## NICOLE

I watched as Barrett unveiled all the food which had been delivered to my cabin as a part of the honeymoon package. I was thankful he had brought the food to me because I wasn't sure if I could even walk at this point, given I thought I'd used up the little energy I had left to get out of the tub and dry myself off. Even with that, Barrett had helped me with parts of it, including putting on my tank top, pajama pants, and a hoodie that I left unzipped.

If I counted the food Barrett picked up earlier in the day and the food we had just received, we, without a doubt, had enough food for us to survive on for several days. The steak, mashed potatoes, asparagus, and several desserts—including chocolate cake—were all I could think about as I waited for him to finish setting everything up so we could chow down. This wasn't including the champagne the staff had already bought to my cabin. This was truly a feast of epic proportions.

"I don't know if I'll be able to move after eating all this food."

"I'm sure you'll find some energy." The fever behind his gaze let me know exactly what he was talking about, as if I hadn't already known. He and I made small talk as we ate dinner. We cuddled up on the couch and watched TV as we waited for our bodies to digest the food. I was more than a little tense as I wondered what his next move would be in this night full of surprises.

Another surprise that had come with the honeymoon package was a dozen red roses, which Barrett had set up between us. Without forcing me to sit up, Barrett leaned over and picked up one of the roses out of the vase. I watched as he twirled the rose between his fingers. I didn't care what was on television anymore as I tried to figure out what he was going to do with it. He soon answered my questions without saying a word.

He took the rose and traced my jawline with it and brought the rose to my nose before he moved further down my neck. Barrett made sure to pay special attention to my breasts, which once again led my nipples to turn into stiff peaks, practically begging him for more attention. It didn't help that my white tank top did little to hide them.

Barrett soon shifted himself from behind me to kneeling in front of me. During the transition, I had somehow ended up sitting across the sofa. Although I missed hearing the steady rhythm of his heart, I was in a very comfortable position. He continued moving the rose up and down my body as my eyes drifted closed.

"You know what I want to do?"

"What?" I responded, not bothering to open my eyes. I was way too comfortable.

"Rip this tank top off of you."

My eyes sprung open and immediately met his. The heat was still in them, but there was something more there. Passion and desire. And I knew it was all for me.

"What's stopping you?"

Barrett threw the rose by the wayside, and he was on me before either of us could say another word. The first thing to go was the tank top he had deemed his enemy. I had to slow him down in order to make sure I wasn't the only one shirtless because I craved the contact of his skin on me. His hands ran up and down my torso, gently brushing the sides of my breasts. How could this simple touch cause my body to hum like a smooth engine?

When Barrett moved to help me take off the rest of my clothes, I flipped the switch, and he ended up on his back with me on top of him with just my panties on.

Our hands were flying everywhere, trying to touch as much surface area on one another as we could. My hands finally got to feel every one of the muscles he had unintentionally been teasing me with under the sweaters he wore at the resort. The dark hair on his chest was not too much yet, not too little, and it lightly tickled my nipples when I leaned down to kiss and nibble on his neck and chest. His hands were alternating between playing with my breasts and other parts of my body as I felt my arousal grow inside of me. My hands travelled from his chest to his flat abdomen down to the place we both wanted them the most.

"Nicole," he said, just above a whisper and with a hint of danger. I leaned down to kiss him, and the fierceness of the kiss could be felt with every stroke of his tongue against my own.

When we broke apart to take a breath, I asked, "Do you have a condom?"

"That was also on my shopping list." He said as he pulled one out of the pocket of the sweatpants he had thrown on after we had gotten out of the tub. "I have some more that are readily accessible too."

"I see you're always prepared."

"Without a doubt."

He gestured for me to shift my body, and he pulled his sweatpants down. I was shocked to find he wasn't wearing any boxers. Although I had felt him grow hard under my hand a day ago, I hadn't been expecting him to be that big. My focus was completely on his cock that I forgot to resume my position, and he was able to climb back on top of me. His hands immediately went to my breasts once more, where he began massaging and playing with my nipples. That temporarily stopped when my hand reached his shaft and was astounded to find it grew even larger under my palm as I moved my hand up and down. He closed his eyes and looked as if he was enjoying the sensations. Up and down. Up and down.

"There's one thing that's missing." The tone of Barrett's voice was enough to heighten my arousal, although I had no idea what was missing. He lowered his head, and I felt his tongue touch my right breast. He drew large circles but refused to go where I wanted him.

"Barrett." I could hear the strain in my voice.

His smile was the only thing I received until his tongue and mouth finally landed on the bullseye. The groan that left my lips was involuntary, and the noises continued as he did his best to torture me by flicking and licking my nipple. His other hand had been keeping my other breast company. I barely noticed his hands were slowly moving down my body due to the commotion he was inflicting on my breasts. What I did notice was the sound of fabric ripping, which brought me out of the haze his motions had put me in. I looked down and noticed what he had done. He had ripped one side of my navy-blue panties.

"I got carried away." Nothing in his voice gave the hint of an apology.

"Are you paying for it?"

"Guess so." He bent down and finished the deed, ripping the other side of my underwear. He tossed the useless fabric aside, and his finger landed just above my core, almost teasing me because he knew where I wanted him to go. But when his finger delved into my folds, I almost bucked off the couch. The rhythm he created as he moved in and out of me only increased the need I had for him, and when his thumb touched my most precious jewel, it was almost game over. He alternated between touching all the sensitive areas of my body, and my body was going wild.

"I think you're ready," he said. Once he took the condom out of the package, I helped him roll it onto the length of him, and he lined it up at my entrance. "Are you sure you want to do this?"

Once again, my eyes landed on his, and there was something in them I couldn't read. "Yes."

With that, he slowly moved into me. At first, the gesture was very sweet, but soon I had had enough. "I appreciate you going slow with me, because this is my first time having sex in a while, but this isn't my first rodeo, and I'm not made of glass." Going slow was the last thing on my mind. I saw his lips twitch, and my heart skipped a beat. My words were all it took before he withdrew from me and then shoved himself into me in one swift motion.

"Barrett!" His name fell out as more of a moan than as a yell. When he did it again, I couldn't form any legible words, and it seemed to only entice him to keep going.

And he kept going. The motion of us moving in sync elicited groans and moans from the both of us I don't think I'd ever be able to describe. I could feel a sheen of sweat breaking out on my body the longer we went.

"Barrett, I'm getting close."

"Me too," he huffed, not once slowing down or missing a beat.

I could feel my nails on his back, digging in, and I hoped I didn't draw blood. I let out a groan as I found my release, and it pleased me to know Barrett wasn't too far behind me. He leaned over me, our foreheads touching, our bodies slick from sweat. He slowly removed himself from me and tried his best to sit up. But even after all of that, we somehow ended up laying on the floor trying to catch our breaths. "We still haven't made it to the bed."

He said nothing for a moment as he tried to concentrate on getting as much air into his lungs as possible. "There's always that possibility for another round."

## FOURTEEN

## BARRETT

Round three came and left along with round four before sleep became the biggest priority. There was one more surprise I had in store, if the weather would corporate. I woke up and noticed Nicole was still sleeping beside me. I slipped out of her embrace and tip-toed over to her cabin's patio. One glance outside told me the snow had stopped, but it left a beautiful coating in the backyard of the cabin. I was relieved to find there was not only a cover for the hot tub itself, but for the entire patio which made my surprise a little easier. It took me a little longer than planned to set everything up, but there was still plenty of time to catch the sunrise, while lying in the hot tub. Once I had the hot tub ready to go, I walked back into the bedroom and found she was still fast asleep. Either this is going to go really well and she would enjoy this, or she was going to kick my ass for waking her up at the crack of dawn. Literally. That was a chance I was willing to take.

"Nicole," I whispered, but didn't get a response. "Nic," I said, a touch above a whisper but still got no response.

"Babe." The word naturally fell out of my mouth, shocking me and causing her to stir.

"Hey," She says as she stretched. "Did you just call me 'babe?'" Her voice was still full of sleep.

"I did." And I offered no more information.

"Is everything all right?"

"Everything is perfect, beautiful," I said, unable to take my eyes off of her. That term of endearment fell out of my mouth as easily as it was for me to breathe.

"If everything's okay, why did you wake me up? We had a pretty late night." Thankfully, she didn't sound angry, more curious than anything.

"I have one last surprise for you."

At the word 'surprise,' her eyes sprung open, and she sat up in the bed. "Where is it?"

"Come on, I'll show you." She slowly got out of bed, and I led her towards the patio.

"Oh, my gosh," is all she said as she took in the scene before her. I had already set up the towels and robes we would need once we exited the hot tub. It took me a couple of seconds to run back into the kitchen and grab the glasses of orange juice I had poured before waking Nicole up.

"If you want a mimosa, I can make it one, but I wanted to err on the side of caution in case you wanted to take a break from alcohol for a bit."

She stared into my eyes for a moment before taking one of the glasses out of my hand. "Thanks so much. For everything. You've made these last couple of days marvelous."

A sense of pride took over as her words brushed over me. "You're welcome. Let's get in before we freeze."

Nicole giggled as I ushered her back inside. "Did you bring a bathing suit with you?"

"I did. I knew the resort had a pool, and I debated going to it. Figured it made sense to be prepared just in case."

I smiled at her as once again, her desire to always be one

step ahead shined through. I walked over to the backpack I'd brought with me and pulled out the swim trunks I had stuffed in there before I left my room. It was another minute or two before she exited the bathroom. It should have been a sin to look as good as she did before the sun was even up. She had thrown her hair into a bun. The dark green bikini fit her like a glove, and the jewel-colored tone made her light brown skin pop even more. My eyes couldn't help themselves as they studied her, almost afraid that if I blinked, she'd disappear.

"Ready?" she asked. She didn't wait for an answer before she headed to the patio doors, the lavender and vanilla scent trailing in her wake.

Due to the cold weather outside, we hurried to the hot tub and got in as quickly as possible. We spent several moments in silence, just enjoying the quietness of the morning and being out in nature without being interrupted.

Nicole sighed and threw her head back.

"That sigh brings back memories."

Nicole lifted her head up and opened one eye. "Don't even go there."

"But you're my favorite subject to study. What turns you on, what makes you lose control, what makes you—"

"Okay. Okay. I get your point."

"But I also like learning more about you. What you're passionate about, what makes you happy. I mean, I'm going to wager a guess that based on your reaction to chai tea lattes, that those make you very happy."

Nicole looked down at the water, and I could see that she was trying to stop the grin that wanted to form on her lips. "Getting to know more about you has made this experience even more worthwhile. And yes, you're right. Chai tea lattes are one of my favorite drinks."

I made a note of it before I could stop myself. We weren't

seeing each other after our time at Holiday Springs, so what did it matter? I shook my head at myself, and I couldn't tell if I was disappointed at my behavior or the fact the end of the road between Nicole and me was just beyond the horizon.

"This is absolutely gorgeous." Nicole's voice brought me out of my thoughts. I looked at her and noticed she was taking in the sunrise, just like I should have been. It was a stunning sight. Relaxing in a hot tub as we watched the sun rise over the mountains was a moment I would never forget.

"You're not kidding."

"How's your back?"

I was expecting that question. "What do you mean? Why would something be wrong with my back?"

A light blush appeared on her cheeks, and she looked back down at the water. "I-I think I might have been a bit rough last night. Can you stand up and turn around?"

I raised an eyebrow at the request but did as she asked. I didn't know she had walked over to me until I felt her fingertips on my back, examining my skin.

"Okay, I don't see any marks."

"What did you expect to find?"

"Half-moons from my nails. I knew I dug in a bit, and I was hoping I didn't hurt you." She took a small step back and looked at me, nibbling on her lip.

"Nope, I'm feeling great." I made a show of rolling my shoulders and sinking back down into my previous position. "Would be potentially up for some more fun in the shower, once you're ready to get out of here. All in the name of saving water."

"Saving water? Is that your only reason for wanting to take a shower with me?"

"I plead the fifth."

With that, a small splash of water ended up hitting my chest and face, and that didn't stop the laughter that left my body.

## FIFTEEN

## NICOLE

"Hey!"

"You got laid, didn't you?"

Why had I let Angie convince me to do a video chat? I rolled my eyes. "Even if I did, what concern is it of yours?"

"It's not. But I'm so happy you did. How was it? Spill some deets."

Just thinking about the night I'd spent with Barrett made me want to call him back here and go for round five. Or at least I thought it was round five. It could have been round six.

After spending the night before last and most of the following day with him because of the snow that fell overnight, I had felt lonely sleeping in my bed last night. That partially frightened me.

"Now, you know I don't kiss and tell."

"Not even to your big sister?"

I bit my lip and weighed my options. I could give her a little snippet of how fantastic the night before last was, but teasing her was also fun. "He was amazing. You know that moment when you close your eyes and stars and fireworks burst behind them?"

"Kind of like what happens in romantic comedies? Yeah."

"Think that multiplied one hundred."

"Oh, he went there, did he?"

I chuckled. "Oh, he went there and everywhere else too." I took a sip of my water, but even though I was drinking something, it was hard to wipe the grin on my face. But there was some hesitation in how I was feeling mixed with worry. Yes, last night had blown my mind, and I didn't want it to end, but I knew it all had to end at some point. So where did that leave us? My sister's words brought me out of my thoughts, sweeping them from my mind.

"Well, I'm glad one of us is having some fun in that department."

"I gotta say, maybe you should have come to the Holiday Springs Resort to experience some fun as well." I made a show of sipping the water I was drinking by throwing my pinky in the air dramatically.

Angie rolled her eyes at me before saying, "Of course, now you invite me to come. Where was this invitation when you are planning the trip?"

"Now, you know you didn't want to come."

"True, and I thought it was a little weird that you were going. But clearly, that has all worked out now."

"That it has. Anyway, Barrett and I are meeting up again. I think we're going to hang around the resort and go to a New Year's Eve party the resort is throwing."

"Did you bring that slinky black dress with you?"

"The one that you used to always borrow from me?" I asked with an eyebrow raised.

"Yes, that one. You should wear it tonight."

I held in a deep sigh. "I want to wear it, but there's a ton of snow here, and although it's beautiful, it makes it very impractical to walk around in a dress and heels."

"Well, maybe Barrett should drive you to and from the party. That way you can look like a million bucks and not have to worry about busting your ass."

We both laughed hard at her comment. When I sobered up, I said, "I hate when you're right."

"Yet, I love it when I am." That sent Angie into another round of giggles. "Well, I'm going to let you go."

"That works, I'm going to work on some words before the party. I'm feeling more inspired."

"Ahem. I wonder why?" The look on my sister's face reminded me of someone very familiar to us both.

"Can you stop hanging out with Dad? That is totally something he would say."

"It's not my fault that saying is perfect for the situation right now."

"You're not wrong," I said with a chuckle.

---

I SPENT the day writing and made significant progress on my manuscript. I had heard from Barrett three times throughout the day, but not nearly on the level we had been communicating on. I was somewhat happy about it, because that gave me more time to spend writing versus being constantly interrupted by text messages. But I also missed him.

I hopped in the shower and started getting ready for the night I would spend with Barrett as we welcomed in the new year. I knew he would be here in about an hour, so I needed to step it up in order for me to be ready on time. I wore my hair down and placed the slinky black dress over my body. I had found a pair of ankle booties I must have stuffed in my bag last minute, along with some black pantyhose. Thankfully, the dress was warmer than it looked. Although I wanted to be fashionable, I wasn't going to risk getting sick trying to do it.

I was ready to go with two minutes to spare, and with one quick look in the mirror to check myself out, I was ready to go. As I was grabbing my purse, there was a knock on the door.

"Coming!" I said as I hurried toward the door. I threw my coat on and opened the door.

"Damn, I was hoping to catch a glimpse of you before you had your coat on."

"I guess we'll both have to wait to see what the other one is wearing until we get to Mountain Lake Bar & Restaurant."

With that, Barrett held his arm out, allowing me to link my arm up with his, and walked me over to his black jeep. Once he made sure I was inside, he walked across the front of the car and slid into the driver's seat. "Have everything you need?"

I felt around for my purse and nodded my head. "I think so."

Barrett then put the car into drive and took off toward the main lodge.

We arrived within a few minutes, and Barrett let me off at the entrance so I didn't have to walk through the snow with heels on. It took him a few more minutes to park his Jeep, but once that was all said and done, we headed into the building. We made a right at guest services and followed a small hallway to get to the restaurant.

Once we were in the restaurant, I could pinpoint how similar the decor was to the main lodge, since the restaurant also included a large stone fireplace, exposed wooden beams, and wooden furniture. The most stunning part of the restaurant to me was the large panoramic windows that overlooked the lake and would also give us the opportunity to see some fireworks without leaving the building.

The hostess seated us, and before we knew it, we were

laughing and chatting it up as we waited for the food we ordered.

"I'm so excited to see the fireworks tonight. I'm sure it will be a beautiful sight."

"But they won't be as stunning as you. You look gorgeous tonight."

I smiled at Barrett's compliment. "Thank you. You clean up pretty well yourself." He looked handsome in a dark green sweater and black slacks with boots.

The evening continued to go smoothly, but I still felt a dark cloud was following us since we reached the main lodge. I knew it was because our time together was coming to an end. In a few days, I'd be headed back to Philly, and he would be headed back to New York City to go back to our normal lives.

"Is everything all right?"

"Yep." He continued to look at me for a few seconds more before cutting another bite of the lobster he ordered and placing it into his mouth. I knew he knew I was lying, but I was happy he didn't question it.

I continued to dig into the salmon I ordered, even though I had somewhat lost my appetite.

Once we had finished with dinner and Barrett settled another bill he wouldn't let me pay for, we walked around the main lodge and chatted with some other vacationers who were staying at the resort. There were also some locals who had come up to the resort to see the fireworks from the restaurant. In the main lodge, Mountain Lake Bar & Restaurant, and Bear Claw Lounge, televisions were set to several channels that were a part of the New Year's Eve Countdown.

"Have you ever gone to see the ball drop in person?" I asked as I picked up a cone-shaped black and gold Happy New Year's Hat for Barrett. I then picked up black gold crown that had New Year's Eve on it for myself and placed it on my head.

Barrett shook his head. "If I had to hazard a guess, I would assume most New Yorkers don't go out there to see the ball drop. It's mostly people from out of the state and out of the country." He placed the hat on his head and gave me a funny expression. "Now I won't admit that under oath, however."

I shook my head at his silliness and placed my hat on my head. I messed with my hair a bit until it was to my liking. A vacationing couple we had spoken to earlier walked up to us again and started a conversation. That burnt enough time until it was five minutes until midnight.

We received plastic flutes of champagne about two minutes to, and before I could blink, we were ten seconds until midnight. Both of us counted down with everyone in Mountain Lake Bar & Restaurant who had gathered at the windows to watch the display that would be shown in several seconds.

Cheers and fireworks went off around us in real life and in our own little bubble as Barrett's lips crashed into mine when the clock struck midnight.

## BARRETT

It was just after 12:30am on New Year's Day, and we were scrambling, trying to find the key to Nicole's cabin without breaking our kiss. We had barely gotten into Nicole's cabin before we were trying to free ourselves from the clothes we had worn that evening.

We pulled away from each other to take off our winter coats, and Nicole said, "Do you know that the smile you're wearing is pure wickedness?"

"Good. It reflects the thoughts that are flying through my mind," I said as I reached for Nicole again, because we were both free from most of our winter gear.

"Hold on. I actually want to make it to the bed this time."

"Didn't we make it to the bed before?"

"Maybe once out of all the times we've done it," she said as she walked through the hallway. I couldn't take my eyes off of her taut, tight ass until it clicked that the quicker I got to her, the quicker we could get down to business.

"Take off your tights. Slowly."

Nicole raised an eyebrow at me but did what I asked her to do. She sat down on the edge of the bed and removed her tights.

I had debated ripping those off like I had her underwear a couple days ago, but was attempting to control my emotions. Barely.

"I've missed seeing your legs, but I've missed seeing them wrapped around my waist more. We'll get to that later. Stand with your legs about shoulder width apart." Nicole followed my directions perfectly, which shocked me. I had gone into this thinking she would be more resistant to this change, but she seemed open to the idea. I wondered what else she would be open to?

"Palms flat on the bed. I wanna see that ass sticking up in the air."

The position Nicole was in led to the hem of the already short black dress to become shorter, the fabric barely covering the black thong I could now tell she was wearing.

I made my way over to her and ran a finger down her spine, watching as she shivered under my touch. My hands made their way to her hips, and I thought about pulling up her dress and taking her from behind. But that wasn't what I really wanted.

I undid the zipper in the back and watched as inches of her smooth, bronze skin were exposed. The dress that had been teasing me for most of the night fell into a puddle of material on the floor. I took my time studying her because the only items left were a black lacy bra and matching thong.

"Turn around," I said, and when she did, that was my undoing.

My hands and mouth were all over her as we both tried to claw at each other and tried to get as close as we could to one another.

Nicole sat on the bed and undid her bra. She waved it in front of me as if she were teasing me with a treat before tossing it. Once her bra was gone, I went to work. My hands and mouth alternated between her breasts, taking her moans and groans as a sign of how much she was enjoying it. I slowly moved down her body and found myself face to face with her black thong.

"Don't worry, I won't rip these."

Nicole made a noncommittal noise, and I wasn't sure if she had even heard me. I dragged the thong down her legs and flicked it to the side. I placed my hands on her inner thighs, pushing them apart, and I inched down to get eye level with her naked mound. My mind temporarily went blank while I got a look at her. When my brain started firing again, I put my mouth on her. That was when the pleasure-torture began. Her hands end up in my hair, her fingers burying themselves in its strands as her arousal continued to climb. I was shocked when a few minutes later, she pulled on my hair, forcing me to stop what I was doing and move back up her body. Her eyes bounced between my eyes and my lips before she smashed her lips into mine.

Nicole turned us both around, helped me take off my sweater, and threw me on the bed, which I happily obliged. I watched as her eyes took their time roaming all over my body, trying to get their fill. She then climbed back on the bed and left a trail of kisses from my neck down until she got to the slacks I still had on. After several seconds of fumbling with my belt, she got it undone, along with the top button and then pulled the zipper completely down. I lifted my hips and pulled down my pants, freeing myself from that restraint. She took her time, caressing me through my boxers before she pulled my cock out. Several minutes later, Nicole was finishing putting the condom on my cock and lay back. I moved between her legs and watched as my cock disappeared into her, releasing a groan from both of us.

"You better not try to treat me like I'm fine china again, Barrett. Set the tempo." Her words were like a roar in my mind. Primal instinct took over as my body crashed into Nicole's repeatedly. As the sweat crept down my forehead, I swiped the back of my hand across my head without slowing down or stopping. When I felt Nicole clamp down on me, I knew it was game over. She went over first, and soon I was following behind her. I took a minute or two to catch my breath before I went to deposit the condom in the garbage.

"I'm still amazed that it gets better every time." I saw Nicole nod out of the corner of my eye, but she said nothing. "At least this time we made it to the bed."

That caused a snort to leave her lips. "True, I guess we are getting better."

---

I WOKE up the next morning to Nicole's soft breaths on my chest. I checked the clock and noticed it was only 5:45am, which was my regular wake up time. I guessed this was my body's way of telling me that soon I would be back in New York City. It meant leaving this thing I was building with Nicole behind, and I wasn't sure how to feel about that.

I gently played with the long, dark strands of her hair that were tossed on my chest. Images of how lovely this felt flew through my mind like someone who was watching a movie on a projector. Never had I craved falling asleep next to someone as much as I did with Nicole. I wanted to kiss her goodbye in the morning before I left the house for work. I'd hold off on greeting her when I first woke up, because that was too early for anyone, I thought as I chuckled to myself.

But that wasn't the agreement we'd made. And I knew I would have to let her go sooner rather than later.

## SEVENTEEN

NICOLE

*Click.*

That was the sound of Barrett leaving my cabin. We mentioned potentially meeting up for one last hoorah, but I didn't know if it was going to happen, since we both were leaving Holiday Springs Resort in two days. That caused a great deal of relief and anxiety. Believing a shower would be the cure to everything, I hopped in, prepared to have a clear mind when I exited. But I didn't. My thoughts went back to Barrett and the great time we were having together.

*But you've only known him for a few days. And this is only supposed to last while you're both here.* Maybe if I repeatedly told myself this, I would believe it.

Once I wrapped up my shower and was dressed once more, I sat down at the desk in my cabin and opened my laptop. The creative juices were flowing, and I wanted to bang out this story. By the time I was finished writing for the day, I was more than a fourth of the way through my first draft. But I still wasn't sure what to do about Barrett, even though I tried to tell myself differently.

"I'm not sure what to do about this." I paced the length of

my room, waiting for Angie to answer the phone. The more the phone rang, the more agitated I got, although it was no one's fault but my own. I mumbled more words as I tried to figure out what was the golden ticket out of this problem.

"I normally would tease you about talking to yourself, but figured now is not the time nor place. What's wrong?"

"I have a problem."

"That much I gathered, because you're mumbling to yourself. What type of problem?"

Before I could respond, Angie interrupted me. "Oh wait, let me guess. His name rhymes with Garrett, and he's fantastic with numbers... among other things, according to you."

"Are you going to continue being a pain in the ass?"

"Would I be anything else, dear sister of mine? But seriously. What's the problem?"

"I might have some tiny feelings for him." I took a deep breath and continued. "But there are several things wrong with all of that."

For some reason, I expected my sister to lecture me about how I was silly for catching feelings for someone who I more than likely wouldn't see again. But she didn't. She said nothing, clearing the floor for me to continue to speak.

"Our original plan was to just have a fling while we stayed here. After all, I'm damaged goods, and he has a rigorous work schedule. We both agreed nothing serious was in the cards, with all the fun we had while we were here. You know, like 'what happens in Vegas, stays in Vegas?' Same thing applies to the Poconos."

"First of all, you aren't damaged goods. Second of all, you clearly don't have those same feelings anymore."

"No, I don't. I daydream about what if we took this, whatever this is, and tried to figure out what it looks like when we get back to our everyday lives. But I don't know if I'm ready to take that leap."

"That's completely understandable. You were about to get married to someone about six months ago."

I thought calling Angie would help me figure out if it were wise to talk to Barrett about how he felt about me, and if changing up our plans for what we were going to do after we left would work. But I didn't know how he felt. I didn't want to stick my neck out there in case he still only wanted a vacation fling. That rejection, on top of all the residual issues that came about because of Chris leaving me at the altar, literally caused me to stop pacing. I couldn't talk about it. I'd rather just let this be a fling versus facing that rejection again.

"Okay, Nicole. If that's what you truly want then no one can stop you."

"I know."

"Hey, I gotta go. I'll talk to you later, okay?"

"Bye, sis."

I had set my phone down on the coffee table and walked over to get a glass of water when it rang. I hurried over to the table and saw it was Angie calling me back.

"Angie, you missed me that quick?"

"I wanted to catch you before you saw it."

"Angie? Before I catch what?"

Her quick intake of breath told me she was bracing to tell me some bad news.

"Chris is engaged."

---

"ANGIE, you've got to be kidding me. Chris is engaged again?"

"It's online right now. Don't worry about looking it up. If

you want to see the social media post, I can send it to you. If not, just avoid social media."

Was I ready to see this? Probably not, but now was as good of time as ever. But it wasn't.

"Look, I gotta go."

"Wait, Nicole—"

"I'll call you back, okay?" I didn't wait for a reply before hanging up the phone.

My first reaction was to turn my phone on vibrate. I was thankful I wasn't home, because who knows who would have dropped by once they saw the news Chris was engaged to someone else. I debated contacting Barrett. But I knew I wouldn't be as much fun to him. Because I wasn't dating him. We weren't in a relationship. So, I didn't want him to feel like I was leaning on him to help me get over the shock of this news.

I glanced back at my phone and saw I had a few more messages from Angie. Part of me wondered if there was any damage control I should do to help with the spread of this. On the other hand, I really didn't give a damn, and it wasn't even that I was hurt about Chris getting engaged so quickly after our relationship had ended. I thought it was more of a shock that had me upset. My phone buzzed in my hand. I looked down, expecting another text message from Angie, but I couldn't believe my eyes when I saw I had a message from Chris. After taking a deep breath and mentally putting my big girl panties on, I opened it.

***Chris:*** *Hey, Nicole. Do you have a moment to talk?*

I quickly typed up a response.

***Me:*** *No, whatever you want to say, you can say it right here.*

I didn't want to get on the phone with him in case I ended up crying. While I waited for him to type something back, I grabbed one of the unopened bottles of wine and poured myself a glass. I checked the time on the microwave. It was 4:04pm. But it was five o'clock somewhere.

When I walked back into my living area and grabbed my phone, I saw I had a long message from Chris.

***Chris:*** *I want to tell you I was engaged to someone else. I didn't realize she was going to post the picture online so quickly, and I hope this text message reaches you before you heard the news from someone else. I wanted to let you know there was nothing you did that stopped us from getting married. I got cold feet, and something in my heart made me feel like that wasn't right. That isn't a reflection on you. It's a reflection on me. I hope this message finds you well. And I'm sorry for any pain I caused you.*

I read through his message four times, not believing what I was reading. Although I felt some hurt from the news, I was pissed. That text message was such bullshit, and the way he handled all of this could have been much better. I took a deep breath before I composed a response.

***Me:*** *Thanks for letting me know. I hope you both have a wonderful life together.*

Screw this. I knew who I wanted to contact, and even if we weren't a thing, I still wanted to play pretend for a little while longer.

***Me:*** *Are you busy right now?*

***Barrett:*** *No, I just got back from the gym. Did you want to do anything?*

***Me:*** *You.*

I hoped my words came across more confidently than I felt.

***Barrett:*** *I'll be there in 20.*

I didn't know how he was possibly going to shower and be at my cabin in twenty minutes, but I also didn't doubt him either. I took my hair out of the ponytail I had placed it in earlier and checked my computer to burn some time while I was waiting for Barrett to arrive.

Although Chris mentioned none of this had to do with me, I couldn't turn that part off in my brain. I knew I wrote romance novels for a living, but maybe this whole falling in love and getting married thing wasn't for me. With that reasoning, it made me happy I'd embarked on this fling with Barrett... even though part of me didn't want it to end.

By the time I started wrapping my brain around that, I could hear the crunching of snow under tires that meant that Barrett had arrived. I jumped up and headed to the door. I flicked my hair back over both of my shoulders and answered the door with a smile on my face. Staring back at me was the most handsome man I had ever laid eyes on with somewhat wet hair.

"That was actually about twenty minutes, I'm impressed," I said, and moved out of the way to let him into the cabin.

"Well, when I was summoned, I didn't want to waste any time, so I did my best." He shed his winter coat and had a dark burgundy sweater on underneath. How did this man look fantastic in every color sweater?

"Is it all right if I talk to you about something quickly?"

"Sure. What's up?"

"Well, let's sit down over here first," I said, gesturing to the couch in my living area. Once we had both done that, there wasn't any way that I could procrastinate with what I wanted to say any longer. "So, I just got the news that my ex-fiancé is engaged again."

He looked taken aback. "Wait a minute. Weren't you supposed to get married about six months ago?"

All I did was nod my head. I could see him doing the calculations in his brain.

I went on. "Look, I'm not going to judge. People fall in love every day and get engaged. Sometimes it's within days of knowing each other, and sometimes it's within fifteen years of knowing each other. That's fine, and it's whatever floats your boat. I'm happy that he's happy. I think the news is more of what shocked me. It just wasn't expected."

"Is there anything I can do to help?"

I appreciated his desire to do so. "I don't think so. I'm just glad you're here. You know, I was a little hesitant to even contact you."

"Why?" Barrett asked. He gently grabbed my right hand and held it in his.

"I know what we're doing is just a fling that is going to end soon, so I just felt a little weird about contacting you about this since in a few days, we'll mean nothing to one another."

"You'll always mean something to me, okay?" I nodded my head, and he continued, "I appreciate you reaching out to me and talking to me when you're feeling like shit. I'm making it my job to cheer you up. Now, you have a couple of options you can use to push your ex-fiancé's news out of your mind."

I had been staring at our enclosed hands, but his words led to me drawing my gaze up to his. "What are the options?"

"Well, we just sit here and lounge, which I'm not opposed to. Or we can see if we can go on one of those carriage rides. You mentioned it a few days ago, but we got snowed in."

"Wait, are you serious, we could do a carriage ride? You know, this is something I've always wanted to do as well. It was something I was going to do on one of my trips to New York City, but it didn't work out." I jumped out of my seat, pulling my hand out of his. "You are amazing. I am so excited. When are we going?"

"Well, if you can be ready in about fifteen minutes, we can head down and meet up with Chapman and Henrietta and Heidi and get the show on the road.

"Who are Henrietta and Heidi?"

"Oh, they are the two horses that are going to be giving us a lift around the resort."

I leaned over to give him a kiss on the lips before heading over to grab my hat, coat, and boots.

## EIGHTEEN

BARRETT

I felt a tap on my chest.

I looked down at Nicole. She pointed to the resort. "Look how beautiful it looks from where we are." She wasn't kidding.

We were settled into the carriage, and Chapman, along with the help of Henrietta and Heidi, started giving us a tour of the resort. Nicole and I were snuggled up in the back underneath a thick blanket and had spent the first few minutes of the ride enjoying the sounds of nature around us. The clapping of the horses' hooves as we made our way around the property. The brisk winter breeze on our faces. Thankfully, there was no more snowfall which might have affected whether or not we could have done this today. Although a carriage ride wasn't the way I would have spent my later afternoon or early evening, seeing the smile on Nicole's face was what mattered.

"You know," Nicole said, before she sat up and adjusted the angle she was lying on my chest. "Even if I could be anywhere else in the world, there's no way I would rather be anywhere else than right here with you."

Her words hit me harder than I expected. "I feel the same way," I whispered back and kissed the top of her head. But that lingering doubt was there as we were preparing to enter our real lives soon. Part of me wanted to debate the original agreement of our fling, and the other part of me wanted to keep silent. I knew how rigorous my work schedule was, and to be perfectly honest, it wasn't fair for anyone else but me to have to deal with that. We were doing this to protect ourselves, which was something I kept having to remind myself.

"Did you want to grab dinner after this?" I asked, looking down at the top of her head.

"That would be wonderful," she said. "Then maybe after that we can get down and dirty."

"I thought you forgot that was how you originally asked me to come over."

"Are you kidding? Who do you think I am?" My chuckle turned into a deeper laugh before my lips met hers.

About twenty minutes later, Chapman, Henrietta, and Heidi were bringing us back to our starting location. We thanked them as Chapman helped Nicole step out of the carriage. Once we said our goodbyes, we walked back to the main lodge, and I brought her up to my suite.

"For as much as we've seen each other during our stay, I don't think I've ever been to your room."

I racked my brain and realized she was right. I had never brought her up here. "Well, it's nothing like the cabin that you have."

"Still. This is great too. Plus, you're closer to food, which wins in my book."

My head swung around to look at her and noticed the comical look on her face. She was trying not to burst out laughing, and by doing so, she wasn't helping me either. When we both couldn't keep it together between the snorts and holding our breath, we both let out laughter that verged on the line of hysterics.

"This shouldn't be that funny."

"I know, but between the look on your face and us both trying to hold it in—"

That sent us into another round of chuckling. I was bent over at the waist, trying to hold it to keep from pulling a muscle. I didn't know how well it was working.

I also knew I'd miss this. Miss hearing her laugh, miss hearing her talk. But what I didn't know was just how much I would.

DINNER WENT OFF WITHOUT A HITCH, and we went back up into my suite afterward. Nicole sat on the couch, removed her boots, and pulled her feet under her.

"This is our last evening together."

I knew it was, but wasn't too thrilled to be reminded. Somehow, I had shifted that fact to the side, but it made sense to address the elephant in the room.

"Yeah. It went by way too fast."

"I know." She pulled her hair, which had been down on her shoulders, and threw it into a ponytail. "Back to the real world we go."

"But that doesn't mean we can't have fun tonight. Let's end our vacation with a bang. I could order deserts and snacks from room service and—"

I stopped because Nicole had stood up and walked over to me. She laid a hand on my chest, just above my heart, and looked me in the eyes.

"I could think of something else we could do." Her hand traced a line down my chest and abdomen until it hit my belt. She undid my belt, unbuttoned my jeans, and shoved them down to my ankles.

"What are you—"

My words died on my lips when she grabbed my cock and began massaging it through my boxer briefs.

"You know," she said. "There is something I've been meaning to do but never had a chance to do."

I gulped. Hard.

"And now I think is the perfect opportunity to do what I want to do." She reached inside the waistband of my underwear and held my erection in her hand. With her other hand, she pulled my briefs down. "Why don't you get rid of that sweater of yours while I work on something down here?"

She didn't need to speak twice because as my sweater was flung across the room, I let out a groan when she knelt down and took me in her mouth.

---

NICOLE WAS BEING MORE quiet than normal the next morning. We'd spent the evening in my room, a change in scenery from all of the time we spent in her cabin. She sipped her chai tea latte quietly as we stood outside of the Bear Claw Lounge. It was one of the last moments we would spend together there. One of the last moments we would have at Holiday Springs Resort. One of the last moments we would have together, period. That thought led to a sense of dread creeping into my mind.

"I had a great time with you." There was a slight quiver in her voice.

"And I had a great time with you. What time are you headed back to Philly?"

"Um." She thought for a moment. "Probably early this evening. No set time."

"Ah, okay. I'm leaving for New York City first thing in the morning. Hoping to avoid most of rush hour, if I can."

An awkward pause passed between the two of us. You'd think, after we had spent so much time getting to know each other intimately, that this wouldn't be an issue, but here we were.

"If you're ever in the area, feel free to reach out."

"Same goes for you when you come to New York City." I could feel the awkwardness oozing out of our words. "Can I give you a kiss goodbye?"

That brought a smile to her face. "Of course."

I leaned down and kissed her, and it was clear our bodies hadn't gotten the memo that we needed to say goodbye. The fire was still there, and I wished there was more we could do to explore it.

"Bye, Barrett," she whispered, just before she walked away.

I watched her for a moment before I turned around and walked into the main lodge without a clear path forward. I didn't want to head to my room but didn't know exactly where I wanted to go either. I found myself in front of the souvenir shop. Figuring I had nothing to lose, I walked inside and looked around to see if I could find anything that my mom would like.

I came across a wintry scarf in shades of the color blue for my mom. Although I had accomplished my goal, something told me to keep looking. I scanned the racks of t-shirts and sweatshirts, looked through some of the shelving that contained books and magazines, but nothing else spoke out to me. I gave up, and as I was walking up to the cash register, something else caught my eye.

A necklace that had a charm on it that looked like a small snow globe. In it was what looked to be a miniature version of the Holiday Springs Resort. Everything in me told me I needed to buy this for Nicole. It would be perfect for her, and I couldn't tame down thoughts of her wearing it and nothing else. I figured I could buy it now and surprise her by heading over to wish her a goodbye.

I started packing up my stuff in my room, because it wouldn't be a bad idea to get an early start, since I was planning on driving back to New York City early the next morning. Once that was done, I grabbed a quick meal downstairs and headed back to my room to enjoy it. I checked my phone and noticed I still had a couple of hours before Nicole said she was going to leave. The necklace was burning a hole in my pocket, and I was wondering what she would think of it.

But two and a half hours after I'd saw her last, when I went to her cabin, there was no answer at the door, and her car was gone.

## NINETEEN

## NICOLE

My fingers flew over the keyboard, hitting as many keys as possible.

The words were coming from my mind and to my fingertips. And my book was coming together—had been for about a week —because I had left Holiday Springs Resort. Although Barrett was never too far from my thoughts, writing had taken over, and I didn't want to lose my mojo or inspiration. But I needed a quick break. I leaned back in my chair and rubbed my hands across my face. My phone had been haunting me for days. It told me that I should reach out to him, even if it was just to say hello, but I couldn't muster up enough courage to type those words.

I finally looked at Chris's social media post. He and his fiancé looked happy. After the initial shock, I felt nothing. I was happy he had moved on and hoped he would make it to the altar.

My notification alert on my phone sent a jolt to my heart. I reached over and snatched it off my desk. It was just a spam email. But it brought my attention back to my phone and if I should reach out to Barrett. I knew I needed to do something.

Now, as good a time as any. I opened the text messaging app on my phone and quickly composed a message.

**Me:** *Hi, it's Nicole. I wanted to reach out, just to say hello. I hope you're doing well.*

My finger hovered over the send button. But I couldn't force myself to press it. I threw my phone down, and I went back to writing a story that was itching to come out of my mind.

ANOTHER WEEK HAD FLOWN BY, and writing was going well. Actually, it was going better than I would have imagined. Although writing for me usually started slow, once I got into a groove, the story took on a life of its own. But my love life post-Barrett was stalled, because he still filled my thoughts. I missed him a lot, which shocked me more than anything, because we had only known each other for a short time before we went our separate ways. The sadness I felt from not seeing Barrett helped feed into the way I was trying to write the heroine and hero of my story. I went back to writing, but after thirty minutes, my train of thought was interrupted when there was a knock on my door. I got up and wasn't surprised to find Angie on the other side.

"Hey, what are you doing here?" I asked. I saw she had come with what looked to be a box full of papers and letters.

"I stopped by the PO box and grabbed all the mail that had been piling up over the last couple of months. I figured I sort it in your living room while you wrote. Then maybe you could take a break, and we can have lunch together."

"That sounds like a plan. Okay, I'll see you in about twenty minutes, I just want to finish up a scene."

"Sounds good." And with that, she sat down on my living room floor and started sorting the mail. I walked back into my office and hammered out the last few words of a scene that showed the couple's rise before the fall.

I headed into the living room. I looked down, and my sister was in the middle of the floor, still sorting the mail. I continued on my way to the kitchen when her voice stopped me.

"Hey, look at this."

"Huh?" I mumbled as I turned around to look at her. She handed me a small box that had my name and my PO Box address on it, but there was no return address. I looked up from the box to my sister. "Are we sure this box is safe?"

The look on her face told me she thought I couldn't be serious right now.

"Just open it."

I quickly took off the wrapping paper to uncover a small, white box. I opened that up and found a necklace inside of it. It looked like a snow globe that had a smaller version of The Holiday Springs Resort in it. When you turned the necklace upside down, snow fell down on the resort. I immediately knew who it was from. I flipped the box over, trying to see if there was a note or something else inside of it.

"Looking for this?" I looked up, and my sister was holding a piece of paper between her fingertips. I grabbed it and turn around, hoping to get some privacy.

*Nicole,*

*I saw this in the souvenir shop and knew I had to get this for you. I was hoping to give it to you in person, but the front desk told me you had checked out already. I hope all's well with you and that you write a kick ass best seller.*

*Sincerely,*

*Barrett.*

I was still digesting what was on the note, and I wasn't paying attention to anything else until my sister called my name.

"So," Angie said, "What is it?"

I turned back around and handed her the box and the note before walking to the window in my living room. I heard Angie gasp. I could hear her scrambling to get up in the background.

"Are you gonna call him?"

"No, well, at least not right now. I need to get this book finished. Plus, we agreed everything that took place at the Holiday Springs Resort would stay at Holiday Springs Resort."

"Well, clearly he didn't get the memo. He sent you this."

"I assume it was because he was supposed to give it to me before I left. So I'm just chalking it up to that."

"Nicole, you're being silly."

"Maybe, but this is what I want right now. To make sure I'm completely focused on writing this book. Now, I'll start on lunch."

"You know you're being stubborn, right?"

I heard my sister talking to me from the living room, but I refused to look over. Sandwiches and a salad were taking precedent over any of the things she was talking about in relation to Barrett and our time together at Holiday Springs. I took the vegetables for the salad out of the fridge and washed them in the sink before I responded to my sister.

"I know I am."

It sounded as if my answer took her by surprise, because she didn't say anything right away. "Are you scared?"

"I mean, why wouldn't I be, given what happened? But I also know that being long distance would potentially be a hot mess, even if he wanted to be together. And as I've said countless times before, my goal is to finish this book."

"What happens after the book is done?"

That question got a rise out of me, and I did my best not to show it. "I don't know where my frame of mind will be when the book is done."

That comment was somewhat of a lie. Although I didn't know for sure where my frame of mind would be after the book was done, I bet I could make an educated guess. It would be where it always seemed to be, no matter how hard I tried to convince myself it shouldn't be. At least it wasn't getting in the way of my finishing up this book. In fact, it was helping to fuel my desire to complete this project.

I threw a glance over my shoulder before I went back to focusing on chopping. "Why are you all of a sudden on the Barrett train?"

"Well, I know how much you've talked about him, but I had no inkling on how he felt. Now I do."

"Oh yeah?"

"He's stuck on you, just as much as you're stuck on him. I'm not sending mementos to someone I don't have feelings for after a fling where there was a clean break."

I stopped chopping again. She did have a great point. But my focus was on my goal, and I would figure out what to do about Barrett later.

## TWENTY

## BARRETT

"Good job, Pierce. This is the work ethic we missed. I'm sure you're happy. Looks like a vacation is just what you needed." Gary was the first person to approach me when I finished my presentation. The congratulations continued as I watched everyone file out of the conference room. At any other point in my life, the praise would have meant everything and would have been topped off with a small celebration at happy hour with some of my coworkers.

In reality, I felt like shit. I was proud of the presentation I'd put together, but the glory didn't feel the same. I would be lying to myself if I said I didn't know why I felt this way.

Nicole.

She was all I could think about, day in and day out. When I woke up in the morning and when I went to bed at night. I wondered if she'd finished her latest book. I wondered if she thought about me as much as I thought about her.

I headed back to my office and sat down at my desk. Normally, I would have started working on another client's portfolio, but I just couldn't bring myself to do it. I glanced at my cell phone with its display facing up. The device taunted me as

I debated whether it made sense to text or call Nicole. I knew she would be in New York City in the next couple of days. It wouldn't be a bad idea for us to meet.

But doubt raged through my veins. We had both agreed that, when we left Holiday Springs, that was it. She didn't want a relationship, especially after she was burned by her ex. And I wasn't too thrilled about having a long-distance relationship anyway, especially with the demands of my job. Those reasons didn't stop her from entering my mind, though. Nothing I did could replace my thoughts of her.

I flipped one of my pens between my fingers, trying to think of what to do.

My eyes shifted from the pen in my hand to the decorative pen holder on my desk. It sat there, almost mocking me. It reminded me of my vacation. It reminded me of the Holiday Springs Resort. It reminded me of Nicole. I sighed and leaned back in my chair, still not having a grasp on what the right move was. I had an easier time figuring out portfolio options for my clients versus trying to straighten out my love life—or lack thereof. The long hours and grueling schedule I had shifted back into my life wasn't cutting it anymore. A knock on the door brought me out of my thoughts.

"Come in," I said.

Colin, one of my co-workers, popped this head around the corner of the door. "Hey, a few of us are going to go head out to go get drinks after work. Is this something you'd be interested in? You should be celebrating today." He was right. I should celebrate today. The presentation I gave was great, but I felt indifferent about it.

"Yeah, I'll grab a drink with you guys. Just come by when everyone is ready to head out." And with that, Colin closed my office door with a resounding click.

I OPENED the door to my condo and tossed my keys on my kitchen counter. Happy hour had been fun, but it wasn't as fun as I remembered it being. It also didn't help that I got hit on by two women while I was there, which served as a bit of an annoyance more than anything. The fact of the matter was none of them were the woman I wanted to be with, which was Nicole Ford, and therein laid the problem I was determined to fix.

About an hour later, I found myself staring at my computer. I knew Nicole would be in town next week. I couldn't just let her come to New York City and not see her. Unless she didn't want to see me. I tapped my fingertips on my desk, trying to hatch some sort of plan about what I should do. It would be easy to just reach out to her. I looked up the bookstore where she was supposed to be having her signing and found her smiling face looking back at me. Just seeing her smile brought up feelings in me which reminded me I should have tried harder to at least stay in touch, let alone figuring out and talking with her, to see if a relationship would work—long distance or not.

I switched gears and looked up her website to see if there was any way to contact her. You know that moment in a cartoon where a light bulb appears above a character's head and turns on and blinks? That just happened to me. I remembered Nicole talking about her writing business, and about how she had an assistant who was her sister. Who better to reach out to about contacting Nicole than a family member who she was close to?

It didn't take long to find Angie's information on Nicole's website, and I copied her email address and began composing the email I hoped would bring Nicole back into my life.

*Hi, Angie,*

*You probably don't know who I am, but my name is Barrett Pierce. I recently spent a lot of time with your sister, Nicole Ford, at the Holiday Springs Resort. We went ice skating, had drinks, dinners, and even did a paint and sip (hers was a tray that said cheers on it). We left on a bit of an awkward note, and I was hoping to see her again when she came to town next week.*

*Sincerely,*

*Barrett*

I read it over several times before pressing send and letting out a deep breath I didn't know I was holding. I didn't know if my actions were for naught, but if I were going to go down, I was going to go down swinging. What I wasn't expecting was to get a reply right away.

*Hi, Barrett,*

*I assume you are who you say you are based on the level of detail. It sounds like you know my sister Nicole, and she has told me quite a bit about you. I would appreciate if we talked versus trading emails back and forth. Let me know what day and time works best for you.*

*Sincerely,*

*Angie*

Well, shoot. I wondered if she was available right now. I wrote a couple sentences detailing I was available now and tomorrow, given that I had the weekend off. Based on how quickly she responded to my first email, I was hoping she would get back to me pretty quickly. But once I realized I was staring at my email for ten minutes straight, I figured it was probably time to find something else to do while I waited for her response.

I called my mom, ordered groceries, and started my laundry. I checked the time once more and figured I had enough time to run out, grab my suits from the cleaners, and be back home before the supermarket delivered my groceries. It didn't take long for me to complete those tasks, including putting my groceries away. When I checked my email once more, there was both an email from Angie and an email from my boss.

The one that made my stomach storm up to my mouth was the email from Angie. I threw the email from work out of my mind and opened the more important one.

*How about tomorrow at 4pm?*

And just like that, the time was set. But that didn't feel like it was enough. I debated what else I could do, and the email from work stared back in my face, begging me to open it. Then an idea popped into my head. I found the closest independent bookstore and checked the time. I still had a couple of hours before they closed. I smiled as I grabbed my keys and phone and jetted out the door.

---

"I JUST WANTED to thank you for the lovely scarf. Too bad it's taken us this long to get together so you could give it to me." Mom and I had just finished up lunch at my condo, and we were walking over to my kitchen to place the dishes in the sink.

"I know, I'm happy we were able to get together though. Don't worry about the dishes." I glanced at my phone on the counter before looking at my mom.

"Me too, son." She placed a hand on my shoulder and gave it a gently squeeze. "Have you talked to the woman who stole your heart in the Poconos?"

I raised an eyebrow before I responded slowly, "What are you talking about, Mom?"

"I know Nicole, I think that was her name.... Yes, Nicole. I know she caught your eye, and I assume you are still longing for her. I can see it in your eyes." At that exact moment, she gestured towards my eyes, making me chuckle. "Plus, you've glanced at your phone fifty million times, as if you're worried about something."

"I think that is a slight exaggeration." I shook my head as my mom shot me a smile. "I haven't talked to her since we left. She didn't reach out after I sent a small gift to her."

"So are you going to do something else or give up?"

"Well, I have a call scheduled with her sister today—"

"Whew. I was worried about what you were going to say."

I stared at my mother for a moment. "Why?"

"Because although I don't know much about your love life, I can count on one hand how many times you've ever brought up a woman you were interested in to me, so I know she means something to you." She sighed. "Things will work out the way they are going to work out, and I know it will be for the best."

I knew she was right, even though I hoped they went the way I wanted it to go. "I know, and I completely agree."

"Good luck," Mom whispered as we grabbed our coats and put them on. With another smile, my mom threw her scarf around her neck before grabbing her purse. We headed downstairs, and she gave me one final hug as Walter, my building's doorman, hailed a cab for her. It only took a few moments for a cab driver to swing around and park in front of the building. With one final hug, I made sure Mom was safely tucked into the backseat of the cab before closing the door. Once I was back inside and I hung my coat up, I walked over to my kitchen counter where I had left my phone and dialed the person who might be willing to help me reach Nicole.

"Hello, is this Angie?" I could give a presentation in front of a room full of people, but getting on the phone with Nicole's sister nearly had me wanting to shake in my shoes.

"Yes, is this Barrett? Hi. How are you doing?"

"I'm okay. I was hoping to talk to you about Nicole."

"Yes. Cutting right to the chase. I like that."

One point on the scoreboard for me then. "Your sister and I met while on vacation a few months ago, and I hope this doesn't appear being weird, but I can't get her out of my mind. We had a blast with one another—"

"In more ways than one." I chuckled at her comment, and then she continued, "Nicole has been talking about you too."

"Oh, really?"

"Yep. If she wasn't, I probably wouldn't have responded to your email."

"Understandable."

"So, you really want to make a go of this?"

"Yes. I want to prove to her I think we could make this work. I've read a couple of her books and—"

"You did what!" Angie's exclamation made me pull the phone back from my ear. It might have served me better on my counter. On speaker.

"I've been reading her books. I picked up four last night, and I'm on the third one now."

"But... why?"

I wasn't sure if I had a clear-cut answer for that. "I was going to see if I could go to her signing and have her sign it for me. Then I got curious and tried one out, even though romance isn't usually the first book I pick up what I go to the bookstore."

"That's a very diplomatic way of putting it."

"Thank you. I had nothing on the agenda yesterday evening, so I read one book. And then next thing I knew, I was picking up the next book, because I wanted to keep going. The way she writes... it's so engaging and keeps you hanging on every page. I don't remember the last time I just read for pleasure."

"Well, I'm glad you're turning into a fan or, at the very least, being supportive. Now let's get down to the nitty gritty on how you can sweep her off her feet while we are in town next week."

## TWENTY-ONE

NICOLE

"Nicole, this is your best book to date. I'm not just saying that because I work for you."

I chuckled at Angie's compliment. It did mean a lot that she thought this was my best book. I knew she was my sister and biggest fan, but she had also read all of my books.

Everything was done, and the book was ready to go live. But there was still a hole in my heart. Based on a number of preorders and the hype building behind this release, I hoped I would have a great launch. I cared about the work I was putting out in the world, and I knew that deep down this book was amazing. But something was missing.

Barrett.

The time we'd spent together directly influenced my latest manuscript. Although my book ended with the couple having their happily ever after, ours hadn't. And I thought about what could have been daily.

What if we lived in the same city? Then again, long-distance relationships worked all the time. But was I even ready for a relationship? Was he?

I pulled my suitcase out of the closet and placed it on the

floor near my bed. I was headed to New York City in a couple of days and wanted to start packing the things I wouldn't need every day.

"Have you picked out the outfit you wanted to wear to the book signing yet?"

I glanced up at Angie as I was throwing a pair of jeans into my suitcase. "No, I haven't."

"Mind if I do it then?"

I shook my head, and Angie headed to the closet. We stood there in silence for a couple of minutes. She rifled through my clothes. I pulled things out of my drawers. When I turned around with a couple items in my hand, I noticed she had thrown a few options on my bed.

"Don't you think these are a little too dressy for the signing?"

She glanced down at the clothes she laid out and then looked back at me. She shrugged and said, "No, I think they're cute." She swung back around and went back to looking through the clothes in my closet.

I dropped the items I had in my hand into one of the compartments in my suitcase and walked over to check out all the options she laid out. "Angie, there is a black sequin dress here."

She stopped what she was doing and looked back over at me. "I figured it didn't hurt to have a dressier dress, just in case. We'll be in New York City over the weekend, and who knows what might happen." I had a few friends in the area, not including a couple of my writing friends that would also be at the event, signing their own things.

I dipped my head and picked up the black sequin dress off of my bed. "Oh, I haven't seen this dress in ages."

"I know, I think the last time you wore it was at Warren's birthday party," we said in unison and before the giggles took over. That dress had caused a bunch of shenanigans that night.

Based on the outfits I had already pulled out of the closet, I knew I was going to over pack. But that wasn't uncommon for me either. I would rather be safe than sorry.

"This is the outfit I think you should wear to the signing." She laid down my pale pink fitted dress that hit just above the knee with a long white blazer. "I know you have a pair of nude shoes around here somewhere because I borrowed them..." she trailed off as she went back to my closet to check if the shoes were there.

"Are you sure you gave them back? Wouldn't be the first time you've 'borrowed' something, and I didn't get back for weeks... or years."

"I'm pretty sure I did." Her voice was more muffled because she had leaned down on her hands and knees and her back was to me. "Ah. Here they are." Her arm shot out from the closet with a pair of shoes in her hand.

"Well, thankfully, I'll be sitting down most of the time." I had bought those shoes as a fashion statement, not because of their practicality.

"I'll make sure to bring a pair of flats for you."

I smiled at my sister. "You're always willing to help me."

She returned the smile. "I try my best."

<hr>

ABOUT A WEEK LATER, I glanced down at the clothes I picked out for the day one more time. Well, no, let me correct myself. I glanced down at the clothes *Angie* had picked out. The pink dress and white blazer were a magnificent combination. Although I knew I looked great, there was nothing I could do that was going to remove the hurt from my heart.

I flipped my phone back and forth in my hand, debating if it was wise to text him. I mean, we could have gotten together, for old times' sake. I was already in New York City, and I'd be here for a couple of days. Before I could talk myself out of it, I quickly fired off a text message.

**Me:** *Hey, Barrett. I'm in town this week promoting my new book. Wanted to know if you wanted to grab drinks somewhere.*

After I pressed send, there was a knock on the door. I folded a piece of my hair behind my ear and headed to the door. I opened it and found Angie on the other side.

"We have to head out now, if we want to be on time for the book signing."

"Let me just grab my badge and purse, and we can go." I backtracked, grabbed the items I needed, and hurried to the hotel room door, letting it close behind me as I followed Angie down the hall.

"Feeling nervous about today?"

"I think there is always a sense of nervousness about these things. It's been a long time since I had a book release, let alone met fans and signed books in public." Angie cut a look at me out of the corner of her eye. "Yes, I'm nervous."

"If you weren't, I'd think there was something wrong."

"Are you going to give me a pep talk?"

"No, because I already know you're going to go out there and kill it. Everyone out there already loves you. I mean, I love you more, but that's beside the point."

I couldn't stop the snort that left my body. I knew this was Angie's version of giving me a pep talk, although she said she wouldn't. I was grateful for it nonetheless.

Soon, we arrived downstairs and were outside the hotel waiting for the doorman to hail a cab. The taxi ride to the meet and greet only took ten minutes, and two staffers rushed me in through a side entrance. Once I was backstage, I peeked from behind the curtain trying to get a gauge of how many people were out there. I could see there was a decent crowd waiting for me to come out. My nerves took over, and I could feel what felt like pattering little feet in my stomach. A few deep breaths and counting to ten helped my nerves a bit, but they were still there.

The plan was to have a brief interview with a few questions from the audience and then the signing would begin. After the organizers ran through the last-minute details of the event with Angie and me, I checked my phone to check the time. Oh, who was I kidding? I checked to see if Barrett had sent a message back yet.

None.

I mentally chided myself. Why did I check my phone? There was always a chance he wouldn't respond and lo and behold, he—

"Nicole, you're on in two minutes."

Angie's voice brought me out of the overthinking spiral I was about to take myself on. With another deep breath, I tried to clear my mind as I waited for my name to be announced.

"Everything is going to go great."

"I know, I know. Doesn't stop the nerves that bubble up last minute."

"Go out there and have a good time. Who knows what fun surprises might happen?"

Fun surprises? This was a standard meet and greet. Before I could question her further, I heard a booming voice across the sound system.

"And now, without further ado, I want to welcome the lady of the hour. *New York Times* best-selling author of twelve, count them, twelve books. She's won a ton of accolades over the years, and it doesn't look like she is slowing down soon. Let's give a huge welcome to the one, the only, Nicole Ford."

Applause erupted from all corners of the bookstore. I smiled and waved as I entered the room. I gave the host a firm hand-shake before taking a seat at one of the stools was on the stage. The crowd quieted down when I took a seat.

"Nicole, welcome to New York City!"

The applause started up once more, and I grinned. When the crowd quieted down again, I said, "New York City is one of my favorite cities in the world. I'm so happy to be here."

"And we are so glad to have you here. I'm sure everyone is ready to get into the Q&A. How we'll do it is we'll start with a few questions we've put together based on questions people asked online. Then we'll open it up to your fans in the audience."

I nodded my head. I received the questions the bookstore's social media team had gathered the night before, so I had already planned some ideas for answers. The wildcard would be what questions the people from the crowd would ask. They had a staffer in the audience who would hear the question before it was asked, just to make sure it was appropriate, but I wouldn't know what the question was before it left the person's lips.

"What served as your inspiration for your new release, *Holiday in the Mountains?*"

A million thoughts flew through my mind as I remembered what served as the inspiration behind my book. I thought about making up a fake story but figured the truth deserved to be heard.

"Well, a few months ago, I went to the Poconos for a small vacation. And I'm sure I don't need to get into details about why I went on that vacation." There was a light murmur among the crowd. I was sure the host wasn't expecting me to allude to my getting left at the altar during the first question. But hey, when in Rome, right?

"So, I went to the Poconos for a minor break, and the place I stayed at was breathtaking. The scenery, the staff, the property itself provided such a magical backdrop to a story." I paused for a moment. I debated going into further detail, but I thought the details of the time Barrett and I spent together should remain between us. "Now I know I've said this before, but I get a lot of my stories based on people watching, and there was a couple there who looked like they had just met but seemed to be getting along well. And I don't know what happened after they left, but they helped me spin a tale of what I hope happened for them. A tale of them finding true love and eternal happiness." That answer seemed to satisfy the crowd, because another round of applause followed.

"Do you have any plans to make this book into a series?"

"I have another holiday book in mind. So, the answer, I guess, would be maybe. It would depend on how I'm feeling about the book series, because I don't like to put out material I don't absolutely love, because I know it won't be high caliber. I guess it's not really an answer to the question."

The questions kept coming like rapid fire. I answered each and every one. I bent down to pick up a water bottle one staffer left near my stool. The question-and-answer session flew by, and I had a couple of cramps in my hand by the time the book signing was over.

I walked back into the backroom where I was before I was announced on stage. I took another sip of my water and opened the door before I said, "Hey, Angie, we need to—"

"Is it all right if I ask a question?"

I thanked my lucky stars I had stopped drinking the water before the question was asked, because I knew that voice immediately. Because it was the voice which had stayed in my dreams. It was the voice in my mind when I woke up in the morning. It was the voice I had tried so hard to forget, but couldn't.

## TWENTY-TWO

## BARRETT

**Barrett**

"WHAT WOULD you do if you made a mistake and let the woman of your dreams get away?"

I hadn't known what I was going to say until I said it. But when I saw the look of surprise on her face, I had hoped I had said the right thing. I still didn't know, because she hadn't said anything since I asked my question. So, I decided to keep talking.

"Nicole, I'm falling in love with you, and it all started at the Holiday Spring Resort. I wanted to give you space because that is what you needed. I'm hoping you're in a better space now, but if you aren't, I'll wait for you. Which is one of the things I should have said before we left the Holiday Springs Resort. The other was the fact I was falling in love with you and that has only grown stronger since we've been apart. You're all I can think about when I wake up, and you're the last thing I think about when I got to sleep. It's been a struggle trying to abide by the rules we set for the fling, when all I wanted to do was travel down to Philly and hold you in my arms."

The silence passed between us like a ping pong match and made me nervous. Did she feel the same way?

She finally made a move and grabbed something that was hanging around her neck. It was then I realized that it was the snow globe necklace I'd sent to her.

"You're wearing it."

"I only take it off to shower." With that, she sprinted the few feet that kept us apart and launched herself into my arms. "Oh, how I've missed you too."

"I'm so proud of you."

"Hmm?" She took a step back to look at me.

"I'm so proud of you. You pushed through all the barriers life has thrown your way and finished your book. I see that it is on track for selling more copies than your last."

"You've been keeping track of my career and book release? How long were you here for?"

I nodded my head. "I was here for most of the questions and answers and the signing. I didn't want to interrupt your signing, because this was your moment, and you deserved to have all of the attention on you. Not only have I been tracking your career, I've bought several of your books at a local bookstore." I held up the four books I'd bought weeks ago and her latest release for her to see. "I figured it would make sense to get them signed since I was here."

That caused a chuckle to fall from her lips. "I can do that and so much more." She leaned up as I leaned down, and when our lips met, I felt the sigh of relief leave her lips. When the kiss ended, she took a step back and looked up at me.

"And I love you too."

"I CAN DO my job from anywhere."

I looked down at Nicole, who was lying in my arms. It was a couple of days after her book signing, and she had rescheduled her train ticket to leave a few days from today. I stopped twisting the strand of hair I had been playing with for the last few minutes and replayed the words she just said through my mind once more.

"We both know you can do your job from anywhere, as long as there's Wi-Fi, but that doesn't mean you should, Nicole. I'm not asking you to move to New York, if you don't want to. I just thought it would be a good idea to suggest, but I understand that that is a big step given that your entire life is in Philadelphia."

"I know, and I wouldn't be strictly doing this for you. I've always wanted to live in New York City. And this is not something I would do right now, but it's definitely an option on the table. Would my moving to New York be a problem for you?" Nicole snapped her head and looked at me as she was asking the question. The look on my face must have looked comical because she was trying to hold back giggles.

"Of course, I would love it if you moved to New York. That would make this whole relationship thing that much easier."

"Relationship thing?" she asked with an eyebrow raised. "Are you saying we're in a relationship?"

"Yes. That's what I'm saying. If you have any objections, then nope, I don't have any idea what relationship thing you're talking about." Nicole let out a belly laugh, and it was then I knew how much I missed it. How much I missed spending time with her. But her laughter brought even more joy to my heart than I was expecting.

"Well, it'll take a while before I can even figure out a move up here. So, if you're game for this, we can use Amtrak to go back and forth and visit each other. It's not that long of a ride at all."

I nodded my head. She was right; it wasn't that far at all. And we could make this work. But I still had one reservation. "Nicole, you know I work long hours, and sometimes I literally go from my condo to work and back to my condo and pass out. So, there might be times where I might not respond to text messages as quickly as I would normally. But I don't want you to think I'm not thinking about you or anything like that."

Nicole bit the corner of her lip before she said, "I know. Sometimes I have to pull all-nighters when I'm up against a hard deadline for a book. And sometimes, a lot of my time is eaten up by creating a marketing strategy that will help sell my book. That doesn't mean we can't come together. Even if it's for a brief moment to check in with one another and make sure everything is going okay."

"You're absolutely right."

She placed her head back down on my chest and ran a finger slowly up and down. She was drawing circles absent-mindedly. We lay like that for a few moments before she broke the silence. "When we were about to leave Holiday Springs Resort, I knew at that particular moment, there was no way I could handle a relationship, but I didn't want to let you go. That hurt from my failed engagement, even if I didn't care about Chris like I did before, was going to harm any relationship I jumped into. But now I'm in a much better headspace. I think the time writing my book helped me get there. If that makes sense."

"Of course, it does. You wrote through the pain you were feeling. It was a creative outlet that allowed you to express your feelings. And now you're better for it."

She leant up to give me a peck on the lips and smiled before laying back down on my chest. "I feel better for it. Without a doubt."

"I missed you." I could tell my words took her by surprise

based on the small gasp that fell from her lips. Her eyes moved from my chest up to my face.

"I missed you too. It hurt visiting New York City and not having you by my side. But I have to admit, what you did at my book signing was pretty damn cool."

"We have Angie to thank for that."

"Do I even want to know how that came to be?"

"I can tell you the long story or the short story."

She lay back down on my chest, going back to the imaginary circles she had been drawing on me. "I think the short story would work for now. But that's only because I'm getting tired."

"After deciding I wanted to try to get you back into my life, I did some research. I was able to find Angie's email, and I reached out to her. I guess you had told her enough details about me that she was able to put two and two together and not think I was a weirdo, and she offered to help us get back together."

Nicole huffed. But I could tell by the smile on her face she wasn't really upset. "Now I owe my sister, and I'm sure I'll never be able to make this up."

"I guess we both owe her. Not that I'm complaining, because you're worth it." I gave her a long kiss on her head, and the scent of lavender and vanilla immediately tickled my nose. The mixture of the two scents immediately made me think of her and increased the calmness I felt about my body. Or it could have been the fact I was tired after the bedroom games we played there earlier.

# EPILOGUE
## NICOLE

**Two Years and Some Months Later**

"ARE YOU READY? WE HAVE TO—" I turned to Angie, and she paused, a mask of surprise covering her face. A gasp fell from her lips, and her hands flew up to cover her mouth. I could see the tears forming in her eyes as she looked me over. "Nic, you look beautiful."

My wedding photographer chose that exact moment to take a photo I was sure would make a beautiful memory. The first time my sister saw me all done up on my wedding day.

I was able to understand the words she said, although it came out somewhat garbled between her hands covering her mouth and the tears now falling down her cheeks.

"You promised you wouldn't cry! Now you're going to make me cry, and we are already dressed and ready to go." I gestured to the white lacy white wedding gown I had on. The off-the-shoulder dress was fitted until the skirt flared out around my knees. My sister was in a deep red gown that matched some of the flowers in my bouquet. "Pull yourself together."

"You're one to talk," Angie said, and she dabbed her eyes. "I can't help myself. I think Mom and Dad will be back here shortly."

I rolled my shoulders out, trying to keep my composure the best I could, but at the rate we were going, that was going to be fruitless. But what did it matter? I was getting married to the love of my life.

"I have a small surprise for you." Angie walked back to a table that was near the door of the suite that Holiday Springs allowed us to get ready in. She rushed back over to me with a drink. "This is from your husband to be."

One quick whiff told me it was a chai tea latte, and I smiled at the thoughtfulness. He was trying to bring me comfort when he couldn't be with me. It was something I'd never really felt from Chris, who couldn't even be bothered to remember what drink I preferred. I didn't realize someone who paid so much attention to detail when it came to me was out there until I met Barrett, and I couldn't believe I'd almost settled for less.

Chris didn't make it down the aisle with the fiancée after me either, but he was currently dating someone else, and it seemed to be going well. I wished him well after he sent me a text message when Angie posted a 'countdown to Nicole's wedding' post on social media, and that was that.

A knock on the door caused us to stop what we were doing. Angie rushed over to the door and opened it, finding our wedding coordinator, Melina, behind the door.

"Nicole, are you ready to go? Small change in plans, but everyone is just going to meet us at the wedding site versus coming here. It made a bit more sense logistically than transporting your parents here and then bringing them back to where the ceremony will take place."

That sounded good to me. Melina had been a beacon of light throughout the whole process, and I couldn't have been more thankful to have her support and help in pulling this whole day together. She'd helped Angie gather everything we both needed, and soon we were off to where my wedding ceremony would take place.

The expansive lands that were a part of the Holiday Springs resort allowed me to make my dream wedding come true, and it was a carefully planned one at that. Unlike my relationship with Barrett. What had begun as a fling, sprung into a romance which was more than I could have ever written.

Barrett and I were long distance for a while, and it seemed to work for us. I would stay at his condo for a few days at a time, and he would sometimes spend the weekend in Philly with me. Those few days I was spending at his apartment turned into a couple of weeks and turned into why-are-you-paying-rent-at-an-apartment-you-are-barely-in, and he asked me to move in with him. A few months later, we were at the one-year anniversary of the weekend we met at the Holiday Springs Resort, and he proposed to me in the cabin I had stayed in. And now, we were getting married at the place where it all began for us.

We had chosen to hold our wedding outdoors because of the beautiful weather that came to Pennsylvania during the month of May.

We were standing behind a tent that blocked me from being seen by the guests. Once we were out of the car and safely behind the tent, I snuck up on my dad, who was waiting to walk me down the aisle. He turned around, and the surprised look on his face was hidden from my line of vision when he leaned over to hug me. When we broke apart, I watched as he discreetly tried to wipe the tears from his eyes. Soon it was time for the ceremony to begin, and we lined up, ready for Melina to tell us when it was time to walk. With my arm linked through my father's and my bouquet firmly in my hand, my father and I started the march down the aisle. The moment my eyes connected with Barrett's was something I will never forget. The love and joy that shined out of them almost made me want to break down into tears. It further confirmed this was it. We were each other's forever.

---

"HELLO, MRS. PIERCE."

I smiled at the man I could officially call my husband. He had just walked back over to our sweetheart table in the Springs View Ballroom and Reception Hall. I was taking a break from talking to our guests. "I love the way that rolls off your tongue."

"Me too. How does it feel to have traded one president's last name for another?"

The laughter that left my body even took me by surprise. "You know what? I hadn't realized that. But Mrs. Pierce has a lovely ring to it. And I wouldn't trade you for anyone in the world."

"Great answer."

I decided to use my new last name in my personal life, but would continue to go by Nicole Ford in the literary world.

"When can we leave?"

I looked at Barrett and could see that he was dead serious. "What do you mean, when can we leave?"

"Just what I said. When is it socially acceptable to leave our reception? Cause I want to leave ten minutes before that."

Of course he did.

"Cool your jets, handsome. The only reason you want to leave is to get back to the honeymoon cabin."

"What can I say? I have some fond memories of that place... some that I want to relive as soon as possible, if you catch my drift."

I did my best not to blush at his words, because I had some

memories I would love to recreate myself. "We'll be out of here soon enough. And then on our honeymoon and then back to the daily grind of the real world."

We had decided to spend the first part of our honeymoon at the Holiday Springs Resort, and then about a week later, we would be flying to Tahiti to spend a couple of weeks there. It was the original beach honeymoon I didn't get a chance to have, but I wouldn't trade anything for the love I found at the Holiday Springs Resort.

Gary, who was currently tearing it up on the dance floor with his wife, Gina, had encouraged Barrett to take as much vacation as he wanted, referencing the fact he had accrued a bunch of time he should use. As for me, my next novel was due to be released in three short months. It was already written and ready to go, which might have been the earliest I'd ever had a book completed. It did help when I had a real-life romance to pull inspiration from.

Barrett reached over and grabbed my left hand. He played with my engagement ring before toying with the new wedding band on my finger. He brought my hand up to his lips and placed a kiss on the back of my hand, which I knew was a promise of things that were to come.

## IT'S ALWAYS BEEN YOU - BOOK #(1)

Next from the Holiday Springs Series
*It's Always Been You, by* A.M. Williams
*Holiday Springs, Book # ( 1 )*
Releasing ( 1 0/23/2o)

**Two best friends and one tiny honeymoon suite…what's the worst that could happen?**

When my ex decided to leave me just three weeks before our wedding, I did the only thing a girl could do. I grabbed my best friend and headed for the mountains to celebrate my newfound freedom and get over my broken heart while taking full advantage of all of the pre-paid amenities that should have happened on my honeymoon. There's just one problem: Holiday Springs Resort is booked solid and I may have forgotten to change our reservations. Now Zeke and I are forced to share a bed, but am I ready to share my heart again so soon?

Delaney always seemed to be the right girl at the wrong time. With her ex-fiancé out of the picture, it's up to me to mend her broken heart. There's just one problem: I've been in love with her since the day we met. With all the romance in the air, it's hard to fight back the tension between us. What was supposed to be a fun-filled rebound trip between friends suddenly heats up to so much more.

Falling in love could mean risking our friendship. Are we both willing to take that leap? One thing is for sure - this trip changes everything.

If you like snowy locales, sizzling romance, and a scene with a hot tub, then you'll love It's Always Been You, the first book in a new series.

**Escape to the romantic paradise of Holiday Springs and warm up with your next happily ever after.**

Visit https://www.facebook.com/HolidaySpringsSeries for all the details.

## HOLIDAY SPRINGS SERIES LIST

Nestled deep in the mountains of Pennsylvania, Holiday Springs Resort promises to bring the heat this winter! Seven amazing authors as they take to the slopes on the adventure of a lifetime and find their happily ever afters. For more information, visit the series website: https://www. facebook.com/HolidaySpringsSeries/

It's Always Been You by A.M. Williams
A Friends to Lovers Romance

Deal Breaker by Julie Archer
A Best Friend's Sibling Romance

Love on the Rocks by Kim Bailey
A Workplace Romance

Stuck With You by Moni Boyce
An Enemies to Lovers Romance

Second Start by S.E. Rose
A Second Chance Romance

Something New by B. Ivy Woods
A Jilted Bride Romance

# STAY CONNECTED

Facebook
Facebook VIP Group
Instagram
Newsletter
Twitter
www.bivywoods.com

# ABOUT THE AUTHOR

B. Ivy Woods has been writing for as long as she can remember. After getting her Bachelor of Arts in Political Science and Environmental Policy and a Master's in Energy Policy and Law and working in the environmental field for several years, she decided to become a stay-at-home mom. That is when thoughts of a writing career really took off. Although she competed in NaNoWriMo multiple times, 2019 was the first year that she won. This win inspired her to make writing a career. Her debut novel was self-published in 2020.

Although she is originally from New York City, she currently lives in the DMV (Washington, D.C., Maryland, Virginia) with her husband, daughter, dog, and cat.

www.ingramcontent.com/pod-product-compliance
Lightning Source LLC
Chambersburg PA
CBHW030750110726

47900CB00008B/2531